Badlands

Badlands

PETER BOWEN

ST. MARTIN'S MINOTAUR
NEW YORK

www.minotaurbooks.com

Library of Congress Cataloging-in-Publication Data

Bowen, Peter, 1945-
    Badlands / Peter Bowen.—1st ed.
        p. cm.
    ISBN 0-312-26252-3
    1. Du Pré, Gabriel (Fictitious character)—Fiction. 2. Serial murders—Fiction.
3. Sheriffs—Fiction. 4. Montana—Fiction. 5. Cults—Fiction. I. Title.

PS3552.O866B68 2003
813'.54—dc21

                                                                          2002037196
                        First Edition: May 2003

                10 9 8 7 6 5 4 3 2 1

For Peg and Howie Fly

CHAPTER 1

Du Pré fiddled the last bars of *Poundmaker's Reel,* drawing the last note out and then fading it to silence. The crowd applauded, politely, with none of the verve they usually gave.

It was midafternoon, Sunday, and this was a party to say farewell to the Eides, ranchers here since 1882, with the graves of their people in a little grove of cottonwoods near the main ranch house. The cattle business had been bad for years, and it had finally broken them. They could not hold on to their land or their leases.

They weren't the first in the country to have to sell out and go. They wouldn't be the last, either. Now they were just the latest.

Madelaine was talking with Millie Eide, who had her arms around her two girls, aged eleven and thirteen. Du Pré cased his fiddle and he put the case on the old piano and walked over to them.

"Thanks, Gabriel," said Millie Eide. "We'll miss your music."

Du Pré nodded.

"Not be so good a place you are gone," he said.

"It's hard," said Millie. "Jeff's heartbroken. But there wasn't a choice. It is what it is."

Du Pré wondered who Jeff was.

Oh, he thought, he is called Bud by everybody but his wife.

Bud Eide was off with a knot of ranchers, all of them laughing too hard.

Du Pré went over to the bar, got a drink, and rolled a smoke. He looked at his fingers, calloused and brown. He was playing alone today, no other musicians.

The news that the Eides were selling out and going was only two days old.

Father Van Den Heuvel was off in a corner spilling his drink on the Hulmes, who were both short and stout and very patient.

Madelaine came to Du Pré and slipped her arm in his and kissed his cheek.

"Too bad, them going," she said.

Du Pré nodded.

"People been leaving here, long time," said Du Pré.

"Quit," said Madelaine. "People been dying, long time, too, don't make it fun. You are sour as old pickles, Du Pré."

"Who is buying their ranch?" said Du Pré.

Madelaine shrugged.

Maybe the Martins, they buy it, add another thirty thousand acres, have a hundred ninety.

"Bart don't know about it, him?" said Madelaine.

Du Pré shook his head.

Bart Fascelli would have bought it, certain, leased it back to the Eides.

But they would not ride what they did not own.

"They should have let Bart know," said Madelaine.

Du Pré nodded. My rich friend, he would have bought it, like that maybe. Maybe I get him, buy Montana. Put up signs. No Golf.

The Eides began to leave. They had several trucks and cars outside, all loaded. For some reason not one of them would say where they were headed.

Bud Eide came to Du Pré and Madelaine, and he nodded once and he held out his hand. Madelaine hugged him.

"Good luck," he said, and he turned away. His eyes were glistening.

Then they got into the vehicles and drove away, some headed east and others west.

Du Pré looked at the sheet cakes and the hot dishes on the big trestle table. Susan Klein began to clear dirty plates and take them back to the big dishwasher, and Madelaine went to help.

Du Pré wandered outside with his drink and his smoke. It was spring, a late spring, and the sere land was raw and the grass hadn't greened up yet. An eagle lazed high in the sun, and Du Pré saw its mate miles away. Goldens, fat on the winter kill.

Bart's big green Suburban pulled in, well spackled with mud, a sagebrush caught in the bottom of the driver's door. He parked the big wagon, opened the door and got out. He picked up the sagebrush and held it in his hand, close to his eyes.

Du Pré walked over to him.

"Smell," said Bart. He held out the scrubby plant.

Du Pré inhaled the bitter clean scent. There was dust in it, and winter.

"Like nothing else," said Bart. "They're gone."

"Yah," said Du Pré. "Why they don't ask you maybe buy it?"

Bart shook his head. He sighed.

"They may have thought it was sort of like asking for charity," said Bart. "Foote's trying to find out who really bought it. A lawyer who acts as agent for hidden investors is as far as we've gotten now."

Du Pré laughed. Lawyer Charles Foote was Bart's attorney, and he made damn sure Bart Fascelli was well taken care of. And the Fascelli money. Lots of money.

"I don't like it," said Bart. "I mean, the Eides can sell their land to whoever they wish to, but it would have been nice if they'd said something, damn it. I would have bought it. It's right next to the badlands."

Them *malpais*, thought Du Pré, where the ghosts scream when the wind blows and the wind is the land, too. I ride out there, the hair on the back of my neck prickles. Something there scares me, I don't know what.

The Eide place, better than thirty thousand acres, was mostly pastureland and poor pasture at that, with some hidden swales where hay and grain could be grown. A good place. They had run about four thousand head on it, shipped calves and yearlings out.

Beefmasters, they like them Beefmasters. That man, down Colorado, he don't care what kind of cow it is, she have a calf, fine, she don't, she is baloney right now. So they look like a lot of breeds.

What they do with all them cows? It is the spring they are out, but drive off, leave them?

New owners bought the cattle, some millions there.

"Du Pré," said Madelaine, "maybe you play a little now, everybody they got them long faces, it is done. So play."

Du Pré nodded, and he went back to his fiddle and took it out and ran the bow over the strings for tune. The A string was a little flat. He twisted the peg.

Du Pré looked up.

Benetsee and his apprentice, the Minneapolis Indian Pelon, were there, just come in from the mud. Pelon's jeans were smeared to the knees.

Benetsee just looked dusty, a neat trick in the short mud season. His running shoes were barely touched. The velcro fasteners flapped.

"Old man!" said Madelaine. "I am glad, see you! You are coming to supper tonight."

"I am not hungry," said Benetsee, grinning, his mouth twisted like a wrung rag.

"I am," said Pelon.

"Him," said Benetsee. "Him, confused."

"The hell I am," said Pelon. "I could use a shower, too."

Du Pré laughed.

Madelaine poured a huge glass of fizzy wine for Benetsee and she carried it to him with the gravity of the Pope bearing a chalice.

"I am not thirsty," said Benetsee.

"Drink this," said Madelaine, "or I get mad."

Benetsee grinned and he took the big glass and he drank it off in a long swallow.

"Not very much," he said.

Madelaine crooked a finger at him.

"You, come," she said. She turned, and her velvet skirt rippled in the light. Her high gray moccasins showed a moment underneath. Her arms and fingers and neck were thick with silver and turquoise.

Fine woman, Du Pré thought. Scare the shit out of me.

Benetsee and Pelon followed Madelaine to the bar. Susan Klein was sitting on a high stool, leaned against the back. Her legs hurt always, the deep scars from the mirror slashing her Achilles tendons stitched and ached after a few hours of standing. She was knitting.

Madelaine poured Benetsee more wine and some soda for Pelon. Pelon nodded at Madelaine and he drank thirstily. She filled his glass again.

"Eides go," said Madelaine.

Benetsee nodded.

"Too bad," he said. "More buffalo though."

Du Pré looked at him. Benetsee put a hand to his mouth. Du Pré sighed and he rolled the old man a cigarette.

"Buffalo?" said Du Pré.

"Yah," said Benetsee.

"What you mean, old man?" said Du Pré.

"Good tobacco," said Benetsee.

CHAPTER

2

Du Pré and Madelaine sat on the smooth log bench he had made for her, under the lilacs in her backyard. The lilacs were in bud but would not leaf for a couple of weeks and would not flower for more than a month. It was sharp cold, icy, and there was a wind. The sky was a black blanket with stars cast across it. They had a six-point Hudson's Bay Company blanket wrapped around them. The air was heavy and would frost later.

"Pret' sad, them Eide," said Madelaine.

"Yah," said Du Pré. He was looking at the Wolf Mountains high and white in the starlight. He pulled out his tobacco pouch and rolled a smoke and then he lit it. Madelaine took it and had a deep drag. She held it for him. The silver on her wrist and hand shimmered.

"You worry," said Madelaine. "You worry about what Benetsee said."

Du Pré grunted.

"Old bastard," he said. "Ever' time he say something, I know I am in trouble. It is like he is fishing. He throw out a buffalo, see Du Pré jump."

"What is that?" said Madelaine. She stood up and so did Du Pré.

There was a faint glow on the horizon to the east of the mountains.

"Shit," said Du Pré. "It is that Eide place burning."

Madelaine nodded.

"We better go there," she said.

They walked round the house and got into Du Pré's old cruiser and he started it and wheeled the car around and he gunned the engine and they shot out of town toward the county road that led to the Eides.

Somebody else's place now, Du Pré thought. He switched on the police radio he wasn't supposed to have.

"What?" said a woman's voice. The dispatcher in Cooper. Du Pré could never remember her name.

"Fire," said Du Pré. "Fire, the Eide place."

"Yeah," said the dispatcher, "we know. Du Pré, you were supposed to bring that transmitter back."

"It don't work," said Du Pré, switching it off. He put the little microphone back in its holder and accelerated.

When they got to the top of the bench and took the road that led off to the east, they could see flashing red and blue lights ahead. The lights would appear and vanish. More cars headed to the Eide place, to the glow on the horizon.

The road went across some foothills spilled down from the Wolf Mountains, and from the highest place they could see the fires, several of them. The buildings were blazing.

"Some trouble, them," said Madelaine. "Burn them down, after they are somebody else's."

Du Pré grunted.

Yah, they burn the place down there they are going. But

8

they are gone before this fire start. If it is arson they are in trouble, yes.

Too many fires for it not to be arson.

Some them Eides end up in jail, sure.

Du Pré pulled up behind Benny Klein's cruiser. Benny was wallowing all over the road. He was a lousy driver.

Du Pré slowed.

"Glad we don't got speeders here," said Madelaine.

"Got none that Benny notices," said Du Pré. No one in Cooper County paid a shred of attention to speed limits except around the schools. Du Pré drove a hundred, a hundred and ten on pavement and a little less on gravel, or a lot less if the road was bad.

Depended.

They dropped down onto a flat and slowed some more. Mule deer were bounding across the road. Benny Klein slowed to a crawl. He'd had a deer come through the windshield of his truck some time ago, and he did not want another deer to do that.

The Eide place was in clear view now. The buildings were red with fire. A roof collapsed and a gout of sparks shot skyward. There were several trucks and cars parked well away from the flames.

Du Pré pulled up beside Benny's cruiser and he stopped and they got out.

Benny looked at the burning buildings.

"Shit," he said, " 'bout all we can do is piss on the ashes."

Du Pré nodded. Everything was gone. Even the metal equipment shed was blackened, the siding buckled by the heat.

A burst of yellow and red and black flame shot out of the metal building. A fuel tank had blown. Benny and Du Pré and Madelaine walked to the knot of people looking on at the blaze.

"Won't go anywhere," said one of them. "Good thing it's wet for the one night a year that it is."

9

Laughter.

"Just as well," somebody said. "Probably been bought by some damn *Californian*."

More laughter.

"I be back, a moment," said Du Pré.

He walked over toward the main house, now a place of glowing walls and crackling heat. Old logs, cut over a century ago and dragged here with draft horses, laid up, chinked with moss and mud at first and later wire and concrete. Take a long time to burn.

Du Pré walked over toward the barn.

No smell of burning flesh. The Eides had left all their stock on the winter range but sold most of the farming equipment at auction. Odd, because the ranch was good only for raising cattle, and without equipment very little could be done.

They either were bringing other machinery, or they had no intention of running cattle on the land.

Du Pré walked between the burning barn and some smaller outbuildings that were also blazing, but now mostly consumed. Not one building had escaped. Only the junkyard, where old trucks and cars and equipment sat, awaiting cannibalizing, was not on fire.

Du Pré looked at the ground for tracks.

He found one. The track of a fuse, laid into the last long low shed. A faint black smear on the yellow-gray earth.

He followed the smear. It led to the junkyard.

Du Pré walked past a rusted old combine, broken teeth in its rakes and the glass knocked out of the cab windows.

He saw a glow.

The red end of a cigarette.

Du Pré dropped down, thinking of his 9mm. It was safely in the glove box of his cruiser.

Du Pré heard soft laughter. He saw a movement. Someone had been sitting in the comfort of an old truck cab, watching the fires and the people who had come too late.

"Peace to you," said a soft voice.

The man stepped out of the shadows then. He was dressed in a dark shirt, oddly cut, with very baggy sleeves and long collar points, high soft Apache moccasins, and dark pants.

Du Pré looked at his face, shaped in the firelight.

"You got some questions to answer," said Du Pré.

"Easily done," said the man. He was young, in his twenties, blond and fair.

"You set these fires?" said Du Pré.

"Yes," said the man, "on the orders of the owner. Now I would suggest you return to your mob there and tell them they must leave. This is a private property. The fires were set safely, and no one is wanted here."

"You do it," said Du Pré, turning away and walking back toward Benny and Madelaine and the others.

Benny was saying something to Madelaine when Du Pré approached. They both laughed.

"Guy back there said the fires were set," said Du Pré, "and we are trespassing."

"Who the hell . . . ?" said Benny.

Du Pré shrugged. He turned and looked back toward the junkyard.

"He was in there," said Du Pré.

"Just watching us?" said Benny.

Du Pré nodded.

"There he is now," said Madelaine. She pointed.

Du Pré looked. It was another man, a dark one, dressed in the same odd clothing. He began to trot toward the people.

The man did not look up until he was ten feet away, and then he slowed and locked eyes with Benny Klein.

"We have no need of your services," said the man. He was a little older than the blond one Du Pré had seen in the junkyard.

"Why the hell set this fire?" said Benny. "These are good buildings."

11

"We will build anew," said the man.

"Who the hell are you?" said Benny.

"You're trespassing," said the man, "and that's against the law. I guess I need to call the Sheriff."

CHAPTER

3

"No, it's not good news," said Bart. He looked grim. His face was very red.

The Host of Yahweh had bought the Eide ranch, Foote had said. A cult from California.

"The which of who?" said Susan Klein.

"The Host of Yahweh," said Bart. "I should have more information by tomorrow. They're one of those Californian millennial sects. If this ain't enough to piss off the Pope . . ."

"Like that bunch of loonies in Oregon?" said Susan. "Had the guru. Ended up in the can for tax fraud and attempted murder, I recall."

"Something," said Bart.

"What the hell do they want with a ranch in the ass end of no place at all?" said Susan Klein. "I mean, there isn't a lot to *do* out there. It's about good for cows and a dozen people, tops. That's some tough country. Hell, there's hardly any water."

"They want it because it is out of the way," said Bart.

"I liked it better around here when it was like it was around here," said Susan. "We got enough homegrown idiots."

Du Pré nodded.

"Hell," said Susan. "You know, that bunch out in Oregon, they swept up homeless folks and brought them to Antelope, I think it was, and had them all register to vote. We haven't got that many people here in Cooper County, damn it, we don't need this."

Du Pré rolled a smoke.

"God damn those Eides," said Susan, savagely polishing the bartop. "Selling to a bunch of weirdos."

"I'm trying to find out how that happened, too," said Bart. "Perhaps there is something to be done."

"It's sold, isn't it?" said Susan.

Bart nodded.

"Shit," said Susan.

Booger Tom came in, limping a little. He'd been kicked working some fresh horses a few days before.

"You hear the news?" said the old man. "All four thousand head of the Eides', well, they's for sale, cheap. Bid and truck 'em yourself."

"Where'd you hear that?" said Susan.

"I got it offen that Internet," said Booger Tom.

"You wrangling computers now?" said Susan.

"Enough to keep track of stock prices," said Booger Tom, "since this fat wop pays me, run his ranch."

"I ain't fat," said Bart.

"You ain't 'zactly *emaciated*, there," said Booger Tom. "Which I hear is all the fashion amongst rich folks."

"I ain't rich either," said Bart. "I just have too much money."

"So give me a raise," said Booger Tom.

"You ain't worth it," said Bart, "but talk to Foote if you like."

Booger Tom snorted.

"Them as favors them Beefmasters will sure be here tomorrow," said the old man. "I guess they's all rounded up."

"How did they do that?" said Bart. "So quick."

"Easier'n you'd think," said Booger Tom. "Went flying over it this morning. Them Eides lucked out way their land lays, and so you haze them cows and put up a couple of gates and each time it gets easier. They was still some hay and cake out for 'em, and so they'd hardly begun to leave for the summer pastures. I think they was all still in the lower two anyhow. Two people on them four-wheelers could prolly do it. They was when we done flew over anyway."

An eighteen-wheeler geared down and pulled off into the parking lot.

In a moment the driver came in, a brown muscular man in his forties.

"You-all tell me how to get to the Eddy place?" he said. "I got some fellers behind me, they won't have to stop. Boss said we'd best be here to truck in the morning."

Susan Klein scratched a few lines on a sheet of paper and she came round the bar and stood with the man.

"Turn there about fifteen miles," she said. "Can't miss it. Just don't miss that fork there or you'll wind up on the McQuarrie place. They aren't selling any cattle now."

The trucker nodded, and stared at the map. He went out the front door.

"That will be too much, Raymond," said Madelaine.

Raymond, Du Pré's son-in-law, had taken over the brand inspections in Cooper County.

"He should call me," said Du Pré. Raymond hadn't.

"You both be busy you are signing off, four thousand head," said Madelaine.

Du Pré nodded.

"That's t'other thing," said Booger Tom. "They's gonna be seven more inspectors here in the mornin', too."

15

"Get that off the Internet?" said Susan.

"Matter of fact, I did," said Booger Tom. "Got your psychiatric records, too. They make some interestin' readin'."

Susan snorted and made the old bastard a whiskey ditch.

Another eighteen-wheeler roared past, and another and another.

Du Pré walked outside. He looked off toward the highway. A solid line of stock haulers was coming on. At forty head each, it would take a hundred to haul away the Eide herd. There would be more than a hundred, probably, depending on the splits.

Du Pré waved back to a hauler, a man in a black cowboy hat. He had a double trailer. The empty rig bounced and whipped.

"But we don't hear nothing here," said Madelaine. She had come up beside him in her moccasins. Silent as Du Pré's father Catfoot, who barely ruffled the dust when he walked.

"Yah," said Du Pré.

"Auction take a long time," said Madelaine.

"No," said Du Pré. "It is done already."

Madelaine looked at him.

"License plates," said Du Pré. "All from Oregon, a few from Idaho. Those cows they are sold already."

"This is strange," said Madelaine. "Couple guys come, burn the place down, then all these trucks. Who are these people?"

"We find out," said Du Pré.

"You be careful, Du Pré," said Madelaine. "You be damn careful."

Du Pré nodded.

Madelaine dug him hard in the ribs.

"I mean careful," she said. "Maybe you don't get angry, Du Pré, you watch out."

Du Pré laughed.

"We go, Canada," he said.

"We live here," said Madelaine. "Our people buried here.

16

We been here a long time gone, Du Pré. These fools, they come, they will not stay. You will see."

Du Pré grunted.

The cattle haulers ground past, each one following the other by radio. They all had big auxiliary diesel tanks welded on the tractors.

Like them Eide never there, this time tomorrow, Du Pré thought. I went there once, they bury old man Eide, down in the grove. Nothing left of them but a graveyard.

Another clot of trucks ground past.

Du Pré sighed and he rolled a smoke and lit it and gave it to Madelaine. She had the one deep drag she liked and then she gave it back to him.

"Come on in, sailor, I buy you a drink maybe," said Madelaine.

Du Pré laughed.

"I am a soldier, in Germany," he said. "Me, out there, looking at them Russians, ready to fight you bet."

"Yah," said Madelaine.

"I get seasick bad," said Du Pré.

"You got them voyageurs in you," said Madelaine. "You don't get seasick. They don't go on the sea."

They went back in the bar. Bart was slumped on a stool, staring into his club soda.

Madelaine went to him and put her arm around his broad shoulders.

"You," she said, "this is not your fault."

"If I had only known," said Bart.

"Some reason they don't tell you," said Madelaine.

"We were always civil," said Bart. "I just don't understand why they would sell to that damn cult and not a word to anyone."

"Maybe there is something else," said Madelaine.

Bart sighed and he patted her hand.

"OK," he said, "I know what you are saying."

17

Madelaine hugged him.

"It work out OK," she said.

Bart snorted.

"It is not country, them," said Madelaine.

"I just wish I had known," said Bart.

"Ah," said Booger Tom, "gives us all somethin' to worry about."

CHAPTER

4

It took all of the light of the day to load the cattle into the haulers. There were nine inspectors, one from four hundred miles away, and Du Pré and Raymond were exhausted and covered with dust by the time the last huge aluminum trailer had been filled, the last inspection form signed.

The two men Du Pré had seen the night the Eide place burned stood silently, arms crossed, in their odd clothing.

The ranch was ashes and tracks. There were three missing head, a tiny loss out of four thousand one hundred and twenty-six beeves.

Du Pré and Raymond stood talking with the other inspectors for a few minutes, and then they left, for they had long drives ahead and a long day behind.

"Damndest business," said one, a weathered white-haired man from Madison country. "At a three hundred dollar loss a head, somebody's out over a million bucks. Wish they'd a give it to me."

Du Pré and Raymond went to Du Pré's old cruiser. They got in.

"Look at those bastards," said Raymond. "They might maybe have dropped from the moon."

The two men in the odd dried-blood-colored shirts had barely moved all day. They weren't moving now.

Du Pré shrugged and started the cruiser's engine and they drove away.

Three miles down the county road they had to pull off. There was a line of haulers pulling halves of prefabricated houses toward the ranch. Eighteen of them, nine houses worth. All identical, white with blue trim.

"Son of a bitch!" said Raymond. "It is an invasion!"

"They got no foundations for them," said Du Pré. "Got to pour concrete before they can set those up."

Then they passed six long vans with dark windows and two heavy trucks piled with construction equipment. Generators, air compressors, gang boxes of hand tools. The haulers and the vans all had California plates on them, but the houses had been prefabbed in Billings.

"I don't like this," said Raymond.

Du Pré drove to the Toussaint Saloon. There were several cars parked out in front, and the usual ruck of old pickups. Some of the cars had Oregon and California plates on them.

"They have landed," said Raymond. He got out stiffly. He would be stiff for the rest of his life after his hard fall, eighty feet.

Damn near died, Du Pré thought, the father of my grandchildren. I got fourteen, I think. Jacqueline maybe hide a few, so she don't upset me.

He hit the steering wheel once with his open hand. It stung. He got out of the cruiser.

Inside it was still. The regulars were lined up on stools at the bar.

The newcomers sat stiffly at tables, the men all in the odd shirts, the women in long gray dresses and scarves. They were eating hamburgers and fries and drinking sodas.

Du Pré and Raymond went to the bar and took the last two stools. The local people looked down the bar at them and then went back to staring off into the distance.

The newcomers rose as one and all of them filed out but a man in his forties, who brought the tabs to the bar. He had a purse on a chain in his hip pocket, and he took bills from it, and left the tip on the bartop. He left without a word.

The door closed.

"Why in the hell did you serve the sons of bitches?" said a rancher, looking angrily at Susan Klein.

"Well, Bill," said Susan, "they were polite and orderly and I had no reason not to. Top of that, it would be against the *law* not to."

"Hell with the law," said Bill.

"Easy for you to say," said Susan, "but I have more difficulties with breaking it."

Bill gulped his drink and he spun off the barstool and stomped out the door. He slammed it.

"There goes his digestion," said Booger Tom. Du Pré looked up, surprised. He hadn't noticed the old cowboy sitting there.

"I think," said Susan Klein, "that we oughta wait and see what they do."

Du Pré heard a big truck gear down and slow. He got up and went out. Two big trailers with earthmoving equipment and a backhoe had stopped. Then the lead truck started and they headed off toward the Eide place.

Day after tomorrow, concrete trucks, Du Pré thought. These people they plan this ver' carefully.

He looked down the road. Madelaine was walking up the

street from her house. She was wearing a brilliantly white blouse and her dark skin and black hair shot with silver shone in the late sun. She waved. Her walk was soft and graceful.

Fine-lookin' woman, thought Du Pré, glad that she likes me.

Me, I don't get mad about this.

Bullshit.

Madelaine got close.

"Not bullshit," she said. "You be careful, Du Pré. Don't you get mad about this."

Du Pré laughed.

Madelaine frequently knew exactly what Du Pré was thinking, as though he had spoken aloud.

So did Jacqueline and Maria, Du Pré's daughters.

My women they understand me too good, Du Pré thought.

Madelaine stood on her toes and kissed him.

"They are here eating hamburgers," said Madelaine. "Nobody throw them through the window, that is good."

Not yet they don't, thought Du Pré.

"This Host of Yahweh," said Madelaine, "Father Van Den Heuvel says they got a lot of money. They sue plenty."

Du Pré nodded.

"They are ver' careful about the law," said Madelaine. "Get a lot of messed-up rich kids. They got a leader but he is pret' invisible. Call him the White Priest. Always wears white robes."

"That Father Van Den Heuvel," said Du Pré, "he is keeping track, the competition."

"That is what he said, too," said Madelaine.

"I don't like this," said Du Pré.

"Nobody like this," said Madelaine, "have a bunch strange people take over."

"They are taking over?" said Du Pré.

"They will try," said Madelaine. "Father Van Den Heuvel he say they have some trouble, California, the White Priest says he will talk, God, find a place they can call their own."

"Christ," said Du Pré.

Madelaine swung her hand through the air, brushing across the Wolf Mountains and the plains and the sky.

"It is yours, Du Pré," said Madelaine, "but it isn't either. You don't own nothing finally but enough earth, bury you in."

"This earth," said Du Pré.

"Somebody else got to do that for you," said Madelaine, "so you don't own much you see."

Du Pré laughed.

Some more vans with dark-tinted windows went past. Du Pré counted eight. All white with blue patterns, like china, painted on them.

"Why they come here?" said Du Pré.

"Why we come here?" said Madelaine.

Du Pré laughed. The Métis came down to Montana from Canada. They had eaten all the buffalo, Manitoba, Saskatchewan. Fight the Sioux for buffalo here. The Métis had more guns and better guns.

"Maybe they don't bother nobody," said Madelaine.

Du Pré sighed and rolled a smoke.

He lit it and Madelaine took it for her one long drag. She handed it back to him.

"OK," said Du Pré.

"Bullshit," said Madelaine. "Me, I don't want them here either but they are. There will be trouble, you know, Du Pré. Maybe bad trouble."

Du Pré nodded.

That rancher Bill, for one, had a bad temper and fast fists.

"It is bad," said Du Pré. "Them things they are always bad."

"They always go bad," said Madelaine, "but this one is not yet. Lots of sick people, people on drugs, living on the streets, they come to the Host of Yahweh, get cleaned up."

Du Pré nodded. It is like that yes.

"I want, talk to Benetsee," said Du Pré.

"That would be good," said Madelaine.

CHAPTER 5

"Unbelievable," said Bart. He was looking down at the Host of Yahweh compound ten thousand feet below. There were neat rows of prefabbed houses laid out in a grid, six large metal barns, and a pair of poured foundations for what would be large buildings.

"A church and a palace for the White Priest," said Bart. "Montana Power ran a quad of 880's in there to service them all. There will be over six hundred people living there."

The pilot looked back over his shoulder.

"Fly the boundaries," said Bart. "It's the map I gave you."

The pilot turned back, nodding.

Du Pré looked down on the old Eide spread from his seat. The land rolled yellow and green with old grass and new grass, cut through with stone outcrops and weathered buttes. The badlands stretched to the east, fantastic pastels of purple and gray and ochre.

"Fencing crews," said Bart. "They plan to run a herd of buffalo. So they need stouter fencing than the Eides had. Pricey. Twenty thousand dollars a mile. Number nine wire and twelve-foot mains sunk in concrete."

Du Pré shook his head.

"Buffalo are the coming thing," said Bart. "The yuppies worry about fat in their diets and buffalo meat has less than beef does."

"They are going to herd buffalo?" said Du Pré.

"I doubt they thought that far," said Bart.

Buffalo, they go where they want. I have seen them run up sheer banks, jump high fences, go where they want, them buffalo. Also they are dangerous. Me, I do not want, inspect loads of buffalo. I don't want Raymond do it, either.

God damn this bullshit.

Du Pré started to roll a smoke and then he remembered he couldn't smoke in the plane, which was a charter out of Billings.

Yuppies.

What is a yuppie exactly?

"Bart," said Du Pré, "what is a yuppie?"

Bart thought about it a moment.

"Remember those clowns who were here back when the wolves were released in the Wolf Mountains?" said Bart.

"Yah," said Du Pré.

"Them," said Bart.

Du Pré nodded. Some of them die in the avalanche, Old Black Claws the big grizzly he eat them under the snow. So they are bear shit, we strain what is left out of the meltwater. It is not much, them.

"One of those barns is the commissary," said Bart. "They truck in food and clothing and all and sell it there."

"You been there?" said Du Pré.

"Nope," said Bart, "they let in the state inspectors because they have to. But no one else. There's a couple of journalists camped out by the gate there. Won't talk to them, won't let them in."

"We can go on down now," said Bart.

Du Pré looked out and down and saw a herd of wild horses running toward the badlands where they hid most of the day. They had been grazing longer now because the grass was fresh and hadn't much food in it.

"Them," said Du Pré, pointing.

The wild horses were running flat out, about twenty of them, with the stallion at the rear and the lead mare out in front guiding the bunch.

"I see 'em," said the pilot. "You want me to go closer."

"Not too close," said Bart.

"Right," said the pilot.

Du Pré waited while the plane banked and then it turned and he could see the horses again. Six of them were grullas, backbred to gray with faint stripes like zebras on their withers. Gray on gray, not black on white.

"What are those?" said Bart, pointing.

"Spanish horses," said Du Pré. "Grullas they are called. They are close to wild horses."

"Are there any wild horses left?" said Bart.

Du Pré shook his head.

"One," said Du Pré. It has a strange name, Przewalski's horse. Or something like that. In middle Asia.

"The Eides never bothered to fence much near the badlands," said Bart.

"No water, no grass," said Du Pré, "no reason a cow go there."

"Some cows would go there," said Bart.

"Want me to fly the badlands?" said the pilot.

Bart looked at Du Pré.

Du Pré nodded.

The pilot dived down a couple of thousand feet and he leveled the plane. Du Pré could see the horses running flat out, and they dashed into the badlands and down a trail that wound through the small strange buttes and odd formations. The horses never slowed.

"Over there," said Bart.

Du Pré looked out Bart's window when the pilot banked the plane.

Four all-terrain vehicles were shooting down the tracks of the horses. The men on them had rifles slung across their backs.

"Those bastards," said Bart. "Look at that."

The horses were safe and long out of range.

The pilot circled.

Two of the all-terrain vehicles were close together and they slowed and stopped. The men on them got out to talk. Then one drove off. The other got back on his four-wheeler and he drove up toward a butte that commanded a view of the trail the wild horses had taken.

The man took a sleeping bag and a sack from the four-wheeler. He carried them up a trail that wound to the top of the butte.

"Let's go back," said Bart.

The pilot nodded and banked the plane.

Du Pré had one last look at the man on the butte, who was looking up at the plane.

"Those sons of bitches," said Bart. "There have been wild horses out there since the days of the buffalo. They don't bother anything that much."

Du Pré shook his head.

"What?" said Bart.

"They fence that off," said Du Pré, "them horses have to go somewhere."

"Why shoot them?" said Bart.

"Maybe they want to," said Du Pré.

Buffalo. There were buffalo here once, and buffalo wolves, and big white grizzlies along the river bottoms.

That William Clark, he say he rather fight two Indians than fight one grizzly.

But they are all gone now.

Benetsee, he will know how long they been there.

Long time gone.

Wonder if them Red Ochre People, them boat people, they were here.

Not in the badlands.

Badlands, they don't even got lizards. Too cold, too dry.

Got horses though.

Grullas. Tough little bastards.

The plane dipped sharply as the pilot approached the dirt strip behind the Toussaint Saloon. He made one low pass. The sheep grazing on the runway fled to a corner of the fenced field.

The pilot made one more turn and then set the plane down, very smoothly, and he cut the props and braked. Du Pré was pushed against his shoulder straps.

The pilot turned the plane around and Bart and Du Pré clambered out. The pilot gunned the engines and was airborne again in thirty seconds.

"There has to be something I can do," said Bart. He slammed his fist into his palm repeatedly.

Du Pré rolled a smoke and lit it and he sucked in a thick stream.

He blew it out.

"Maybe not," said Du Pré. "I don't think them horses, protected."

"I don't like this," said Bart.

"Nobody like it," said Du Pré. "So far they done nothing."

Bart screwed up his big red face.

"They will," he said.

Du Pré nodded.

He began to walk toward the saloon and Bart fell in behind. Madelaine was behind the bar, stringing beads on her threaded needle. Her tongue poked out of the corner of her mouth.

Du Pré slid up on a barstool.

"Don't do this you are older'n Saint Jean's shit," said Madelaine. She half-closed one eye.

"They are going, shoot the wild horses," said Du Pré.

Madelaine got the bead on the needle and she put it on to the little purse she was making beautiful.

She put down the purse and she got a drink for Du Pré.

"Go, see Benetsee," she said.

CHAPTER

6

Du Pré drove the old cruiser up the rutted track that led to Benetsee's cabin. The house stood dark and empty, dead. The old man's old dogs had died years before.

Du Pré parked the cruiser and he opened the trunk and took out a jug of screwtop wine and a sack of food, cooked meat and potatoes and bread and jars of preserves, that Madelaine had sent along.

Du Pré walked back past the cabin and down the little dip that led to the meadow where Benetsee's sweat lodge stood. The flap was up and the sweat lodge empty.

Du Pré saw a movement at the corner of his eye. A skunk, bold black and white, secure in its stinks. The little animal wandered past the sweat lodge, nose to the ground. It flipped up a cowpie and snapped at something, and then it went on toward the creek and was lost in the willows. The faint smell of its perfume wafted to Du Pré.

A kingfisher shot past, *skraaaking* loudly. The bird flew down the creek and then it turned and flew back and dived and landed on a branch. The iridescent blue of its back and head flashed in the sun.

Then a cloud blocked the light and the earth went gray. Mosquitoes held in the shade by the sunlight rose up from their hiding places. They would be pretty bad this spring, and it wouldn't get better till the soil dried out.

Du Pré set the wine and the food down on a stump and he sat on a polished cottonwood log. He rolled a smoke and lit it and he had a drink of whiskey from his flask.

The kingfisher flew past again and went out of sight down the stream.

Du Pré sighed.

"Old man, I got, talk you," he shouted.

Something rustled in the bushes and Du Pré saw the yellow-gray fur of a coyote flash past.

Then silence.

Du Pré put his head in his hands. It had ached all morning.

Something hit him in the back, like a June beetle.

Du Pré smelled woodsmoke. He started. He turned around. Nothing.

The kingfisher flew past again, *skraaack skraaack.*

Du Pré got another smell of woodsmoke.

He sighed and stood up. He went to the firepit and found that the fire and the stones were already laid up. He flicked his lighter at the paper in the bottom of the little trench and the fire caught quickly and it soon was roaring, the pitchy knots in the split wood popping loudly.

The rick collapsed and the stones sat down on red-hot coals. Du Pré watched them until they had a faint white patina, and then he got the shovel and he carried them to the sweat lodge and set them in the pit. He went to the creek and filled the little bucket with water and he put that inside the sweat lodge and then he stripped and got in and he pulled the flap down and the stones glowed faint red in the dark.

Du Pré sloshed water on them and steam exploded and the air in the lodge was thick and heavy and hot and pitch-black.

Du Pré sang, old songs, some of the songs he knew but not what the words meant. Benetsee had never told him.

The steam faded and Du Pré put on more water and another burst of wet and hot filled his lungs and touched his skin.

"Old bastard," sang Du Pré. "You old goat, you tell me, yes, what do I do now. Tell me about the horses. Tell me about the Host of Yah-Hoo or whoever the hell they are."

The heat was heavy and Du Pré began to choke. He threw open the flap and crawled out of the lodge and he ran to the creek and the big pool and he jumped in. The shock of the cold water felt very good.

Then the cold went from his hot skin to his bones and Du Pré made the bank and he slipped out and stood shivering a moment. The wind dried him rapidly.

He turned to walk back to his clothes.

A woman in a long gray dress was standing by Benetsee's cabin, and a man in the odd full shirt of the Host of Yahweh was walking down the little incline toward Du Pré.

Du Pré pulled on his clothes and sat on the stump to pull on his boots.

The man stopped a few feet away.

Du Pré looked at him.

"We came to see the medicine man," said the man.

"Not here," said Du Pré. "And you go now and you don't never come back here."

Du Pré stood up.

Then the woman screamed and Du Pré and the man looked back up the little hillock, to see her pushing frantically at something on her leg.

Black and white.

The skunk.

The woman screamed again and the skunk let go of her and it waddled under Benetsee's house.

Du Pré smiled.

The couple left. Du Pré heard an engine start and then a truck back and fill and go down the rutted drive.

Son of a bitch. That skunk act OK but maybe it is rabid.

Du Pré felt something hit him in the back again. He turned and he looked down.

A fir cone, from the one tree that grew behind Benetsee's cabin. A giant from a forest long gone, the Douglas fir was more than a hundred feet high and that after lightning had cropped the top.

Du Pré looked up.

Benetsee was sitting on a limb fifty feet up, grinning.

"Old son of a bitch!" said Du Pré. "I am here, I bring you wine and good food, I am lucky you don't shit on me I guess."

"You don't get under the tree right," said Benetsee.

"I thought you maybe were the skunk," said Du Pré.

Benetsee laughed and he shook his head.

"Just a skunk," he said. "Lives around here. Got a family, a home, pret' good fellow that skunk."

Du Pré laughed.

"You maybe break your damn neck getting down, there," he said. He looked away at the creek. The kingfisher flew past again.

Du Pré sat down on the stump again and he rolled two smokes and lit one. He had another mouthful of whiskey from his flask.

He raised his head slowly and looked at the branch, which was now unoccupied.

"You piss me off one time, old man," said Du Pré, "I maybe just shoot you. I say, the judge, you see I had to do that, shoot him."

Benetsee farted loudly, behind Du Pré.

"Where is that Pelon?" said Du Pré.

"Home," said Benetsee. "He got a family, wife, like that skunk."

"Why that skunk bite that woman?"

Du Pré looked at Benetsee, who grinned.

"Ask that skunk, him," said Benetsee.

Du Pré snorted and looked down.

The skunk was sitting between his feet, looking up at him.

"God damn you," said Du Pré.

The skunk cocked its head and Du Pré watched its beady little eyes.

"Ask," said Benetsee.

"Why you bite that woman," said Du Pré to the skunk.

The skunk shrugged and turned and walked off toward the creek.

Du Pré watched the trouble end of the skunk go.

"Ver' funny," said Du Pré.

"Him nice skunk," said Benetsee. "Just don't like strangers. You maybe buy him a drink, you can bitch each other."

Du Pré sighed.

"Susan Klein like that," said Du Pré.

Benetsee pulled a little saucer out of the pocket of his dirty pants and he put it on the ground by Du Pré.

He took the top off the wine and poured the saucer full.

"Crazy," said Du Pré.

The skunk came out from behind the stump and it licked happily at the fizzy pink wine.

"Christ," said Du Pré, "he get drunk maybe he wants, fight."

"Skunks don't fight," said Benetsee. "Don't have to."

Du Pré nodded.

"The horses," said Du Pré, "them Host of Yahweh people, they will kill the horses, run the badlands now."

"We sweat," said Benetsee.

Du Pré went to the stump that had the axe buried in it. He began to split wood for a new stone rick.

CHAPTER

7

"Skunk take a chunk out of her," said Madelaine. "It was not rabid, Du Pré."

"No," said Du Pré, "crazy. That old man he is talking, the skunk. Drive the skunk crazy. Drive me crazy, too. He is like that, you know."

"You bitch 'bout Benetsee all the time," said Madelaine. "It is good for you. Keep the fat out of your blood."

"Any of them come in today?" said Du Pré.

"No," said Madelaine. "Quit talking, me." She stuck her tongue out of the corner of her mouth. Her eyes were nearly squinted shut.

"Maybe you get glasses," said Du Pré.

"Read a poem once," said Madelaine, "said girls, glasses, they don't get fucked much."

"I fuck you you get glasses," said Du Pré.

"Nice of you," said Madelaine. "I want some, got them wings on them, all covered, rhinestones."

Du Pré snorted.

"Don't like them rhinestones?" said Madelaine. "I think maybe they classy, you know."

Du Pré fished his reading glasses out of his shirt pocket and handed them to Madelaine.

"What is this shit," she said, "no rhinestones, no wings." She put them on and she looked at the needle and the beads.

She looked at Du Pré.

"Gabriel!" she said, "I have not seen you for years! Miracle! I call Father Van Den Heuvel, tell him, maybe this saloon it is a shrine. Make big money off the pilgrims."

Du Pré snorted.

"Burn all the crutches, the woodstove, the winter," said Madelaine. "You don't got, cut so much wood."

"They got reading glasses, the store in Cooper," said Du Pré. "Got all kinds you know. They are some stronger than others."

Madelaine looked over the tops of the frames at Du Pré.

"These are fine," she said. "They are the right ones."

Du Pré gestured and she handed them to him. He squinted and he tried to see the little magnification number on the earpiece.

"Son of a bitch," said Du Pré. "I cannot see that damn number. I need the glasses. Can't see it if they are on my head."

"Take 'em with you," said Madelaine. "You can get another pair look at this one."

"I am going, glasses now?" said Du Pré.

Madelaine stuck her finger with the needle and she ripped off a long string of curses, in ladylike tones.

" 'Less you want I bleed to fucking death," she said. She sucked her finger.

"Give me that needle," said Du Pré. "You hurt yourself."

"Go get glasses," said Madelaine. "I wait till you get back. I got all little holes in my finger." She held out her left forefinger. It was swollen and abused.

Du Pré finished his drink and he got off the stool and went out, rolling a smoke as he walked. He got in the old cruiser and started it and he turned around and headed off the thirty miles to Cooper, the county seat.

It was a beautiful day now, with only a few white puffs high up and some cirrus to the west.

Du Pré turned on the blacktop and gunned the engine and he was soon going a hundred over the rolling prairie. He slowed to fifty at the tops of hills, in case there was one of the huge tractors lumbering down the highway.

The grass was greening up. Snipe flew up from the little wetlands and the meadowlarks trilled from fence posts. The air had a taste of snow yet. There was a fresh white blanket on the peaks of the Wolf Mountains.

Roaring downhill on a long stretch Du Pré pulled out and passed two of the big vans that the Host of Yahweh owned. Both had California plates, and dark-tinted windows. Du Pré couldn't see a thing in the vans at all.

He slowed at the top of the hill until he could see it was clear and then he gunned the engine and shot down a long stretch. The road wound up the rolling prairie on the far side, a snaky and treacherous highway. The hill was higher than it looked.

Du Pré threaded his way through the turns and when he got to the top he could see Cooper five miles away, the metal roofs of the houses shining silver in the sun.

Du Pré slowed when he came near the school at the west end of the town. He went by at twenty miles an hour. Little blisters were at recess, screaming and yelling and beating the crap out of each other.

That Bodine kid used to pound me up pret' good, thought Du Pré, he was bigger. One day Catfoot he is walking by, sees it, takes me outside that evening, says, you box like *this*. We practice. I bust the Bodine kid's nose and he leave me alone after that.

Kids.

Du Pré turned into the muddy lot by the general store and he got out and picked his way past the worst of the puddles. There was a boot scraper by the door and he knocked off most of the mud on that, then shuffled on the scrub mat a while. Then he went in. There was no one in the place but the woman at the checkout counter. She was putting packs of cigarettes in the rack.

"Hi, Du Pré," she said. "Madelaine called, said to tell you get some with rhinestones."

Du Pré fished his reading glasses out of his pocket.

"You maybe see what the number is on this?" he said. The woman nodded and she took them.

"One-seventy-five," she said. "I dunno how many of them we got with rhinestones. Prolly have to go to the Wal-Mart in Billings."

Du Pré went back to the rack of reading glasses that stood in the aisle with the barrels of horseshoes and the overalls and the Carhartt work clothing.

He looked through the glasses. None of them had wings on them, let alone rhinestones. He took three pairs of one-seventy-fives and he went to the little section of shelf that had hobby stuffs on it. He got a tube of superglue and a small bag of blue rhinestone beads. He got a thin whippy plastic ruler from the school supplies.

He set his purchases down on the counter.

"Madelaine said if there weren't ones with rhinestones on them not to be an asshole," said the cashier.

"I cannot help it, me," said Du Pré.

"Well," said the woman, "I told ya. Ya gotta give me that." She rang up the purchases, which came to twenty-four dollars and ninety-three cents.

"You want a bag?" said the woman.

Du Pré went out to his cruiser and got in and fished a pair of scissors out of the glove box. He cut out two wings and stuck the blue rhinestone beads on them with the superglue. Then he stuck the wings on a pair of glasses. They were uneven and they went a good four inches out from the sides.

The two vans he had passed turned in to the parking lot. They stopped and the front doors opened and two men and two women got out, the men in the odd shirts, the women in the long gray dresses and high boots.

One of the men was the blond man Du Pré had spoken with the night the Eide place burned.

The four went in to the front door of the general store.

Du Pré rolled a smoke and lit it. He got out and tried one of the doors on the van nearest to him, but it was locked. He got back in his cruiser and he turned out on to the street and went slowly past the school.

The children were back inside, suffering from education.

Du Pré gunned the engine and shot down the highway, slowing at the hilltops and making up time on the downslopes. He fished his big flask out from under the seat and had a snort.

In the sweat lodge I dream, horses, thought Du Pré, wild horses and the buffalo, on the hills. The horses are all grullas. The buffalo all have blue hides. There are no people.

When the buffalo and the horses run into the badlands they go to ghosts. You can see through them.

Benetsee singing in words I do not know.

People dancing around a fire, waving bloody pieces of meat. Buffalo meat.

We live, they sing, through another winter.

I dream I am riding a grulla and I am very small, I am standing on the horse's back, holding a few strands of hair.

Riding into the badlands.

Benetsee singing.

Horse running hard.

41

I see a woman on a butte, dressed in white deerskins.

The woman jumps over the edge of the butte and she falls like a willow leaf, turning, turning, over and over.

I am on the horse and we go into a narrow place in the trail.

When I come out the woman is gone and I cannot see her.

I look up and there she is standing on top again, and I turn my head and she falls again.

Like a willow leaf.

Over and over.

CHAPTER

8

"Ver' nice glasses," said Pallas. "Them wings make you like a birdhead. Grandpère make them for you?"

"Yes," said Madelaine.

"I bust his chops," said Pallas, "for being smart-ass."

"I will," said Madelaine. She looked at Du Pré sleepily.

They were having dinner with Raymond and Jacqueline and their herd of children.

"You got more you are not telling me about?" said Du Pré to his daughter.

"No, Papa," said Jacqueline. "I don't hide them from you. You are a strong grandpère. You know all of their names, too, but it is all right you want to make us think that you don't."

"How is your boyfriend?" said Madelaine, looking at Pallas.

"Ripper?" said Pallas. "Oh, he thinks I am a kid, so he don't call so much. He will get over it." Ripper was an FBI agent back in Washington D.C., and had fled Montana in terror of Pallas.

Du Pré roared with laughter.

Pallas grinned at him.

"You wait," she said. "That Ripper he is a stupid son of a bitch but I love him, save him from himself."

More laughter.

"Just wait," said Pallas. "You got money, you put it down, there."

"When you marrying him?" said Madelaine.

"I am sixteen," said Pallas, "then I marry him."

"You got to have my permission," said Raymond.

Pallas looked at him with true pity in her eyes.

"I will get," she said, "your goddamn permission."

Madelaine smiled at Pallas.

"Come here," she said. Pallas got up and went to Madelaine and got in Madelaine's lap.

"What?" said Pallas.

"You really want that Ripper?" said Madelaine.

Pallas nodded.

"OK," said Madelaine. "I help you get him."

Oh, good, thought Du Pré, I get a really crazy bastard, grandson-in-law.

"Good," said Pallas.

"Now," said Madelaine, leaning over so she could whisper in Pallas's ear, and she did.

The little girl listened and she grinned.

"He ain't got a chance," said Raymond. "None of us ever had a chance."

"You had plenty chances," said Jacqueline. "Good thing for you you don't take them."

Du Pré looked at Madelaine and she looked back at him.

"I go now," he said.

Du Pré nodded and Madelaine made her mouth into a kiss and then she turned back to Pallas, who was whispering away a mile a minute.

Du Pré got into his cruiser and started it, rolled a smoke and lit it.

It was coming on dark and would be a moonless night.

He turned out on to the street and drove off toward the Eide place. He stopped on the last high hill before the turnoff on the county road that led to the huge log gate. The new settlement glowed with lights. There were high poles with mercury lamps in them casting their pale green glow.

Du Pré went down a side road and opened a gate and closed it and went on, with no headlights. The road was a gray ribbon in darker earth. It was a bad one, potholed and with stones weathered out of the center. A couple of times he had to put one set of tires on the grass and ride the other on the stones so he would not tear out his oil pan and transmission.

The road snaked back through some old waterways and outwash plains to the very eastern edge of the Wolf Mountain rise. The foothills came down and flattened. Du Pré was just below them, out of sight.

He found a shadowed place in the trees and left the cruiser. He tucked the 9mm in its holster and put it on its rigging and slid it on, the heavy pistol under his left arm. He went to the trunk and took out his old Winchester .270. He looked through the light-gathering telescopic sight. He could make out quite a lot at four-power magnification.

Du Pré stopped and looked up at the stars for a moment and then he began to trot up the trail that wound to the benchlands that the Wolf Mountains sat on.

Du Pré came round a scarp of rock and he could see the little butte that the man had gone up on in the morning three-quarters of a mile away.

Du Pré kept on trotting. He moved from shadow to shadow. His old rifle had not a speck of gleam on it and the lenses of the telescopic sight were capped. He looked down at the path, watching for rock slides and other noisemakers.

A little wind kicked up and soughed in the sagebrush.

Off in the badlands it screamed.

Du Pré got to the edge of the benchlands. The little butte was only a quarter mile away.

Du Pré found some rocks he liked and he sat. He rolled a smoke and lit it with his back turned to the butte and then he cupped the cigarette in his hand so that the glow would be invisible more than twenty feet away.

Du Pré relaxed and finished his smoke, then he put it out and took out his little flask and had some whiskey and then he took the lens caps off the telescopic sight on his rifle.

He sighted on the line that led to the place that the man had been in the morning.

He was still there, a shadow, but one that moved. He stood up and he stretched. Du Pré could see him fairly clearly. He reached for the dial and he moved the magnification up.

NineX was as high as the sight went, but Du Pré lost detail when the magnification was that powerful. He backed it down to four. He could see the man pretty clearly.

Du Pré bedded the rifle on two pieces of dead juniper and then he sat back and looked up at the stars. The Gourd had moved to eleven o'clock.

The horses would be coming soon. Coming down the trail for grass and for water, out of the badlands.

A light flashed on the top of the butte and Du Pré put the sight to his eye.

The man had a flashlight on, a small one, and he was looking for something. The light stopped and Du Pré could see the rifle, a black nylon stock and a stainless steel barrel, propped against a rock.

Du Pré breathed in and let out his breath and squeezed the trigger and closed his eyes the instant the gun fired.

The recoil pushed the rifle and sight up, and it took a moment for Du Pré to find the man on the butte again. The flashlight was out, but there was so little cover there that the man, flat down on the ground, stood out because he was darker than the rocks and a little below Du Pré.

Du Pré heard the stallion scream and the sound of hooves drumming on hard earth.

The horses broke out of the shadow of the butte, well past the man who had been waiting with his rifle.

Du Pré stood up.

He looked once again through the sight. The man was gone.

Du Pré began to walk back to his cruiser. He hadn't gone very far when he heard the scream of the little engine on the four-wheeler.

Du Pré picked up his speed. He stopped and listened.

He couldn't tell where the thing was.

Du Pré trotted on.

He paused in a shadow beneath a big rock.

The engine screamed below.

The man was brave. He was coming to look for whoever had shot at him.

Du Pré cursed and he took some parachute cord out of his pocket. He went to the wash that led from the bench down to the land below. He tied one end to a live juniper, a thick healthy one, and he scrambled across the wash to the other side.

This was the only way up. I think.

In a moment Du Pré could see the little headlights of the four-wheeler. It was screaming up the wash.

Du Pré belayed the cord around another juniper, and then he let it down slowly, till it was about three feet off the ground.

The man on the four-wheeler turned off the little headlights. He had to slow down, because the scree and shale were slippery and the machine did not do well at a higher speed.

The man hit the parachute cord, not very hard, but it went under his chin and jerked him back. He tumbled off the four-wheeler and the machine came to a stop.

Du Pré scrambled down the side of the wash.

The man was trying to sit up, and then he rolled a couple of times downhill.

Du Pré put the 9mm against the engine of the offroad vehicle and he pulled the trigger three times. The bullets broke the aluminum engine.

The man was still trying to sit up.

Du Pré clubbed him once with the butt of the 9mm.

CHAPTER

9

Du Pré stopped a mile or so before he came to the main road. He got out and opened the trunk. He took out the .270 and put the 9mm in the case with it and then he slid the case into a cleft in a rock that faced away from the road. He cut a juniper branch and he wedged it in the cleft.

From ten feet away you could never see the case, even with the flashlight Du Pré was pointing right at it.

He took his other 9mm from its case and he put it in the holster. He took off the light gloves he had been wearing and he rolled a smoke and lit it and he stood on top of the rock and looked south.

Lights set on dim moved up the main road and they stopped by the fork where the back road Du Pré was on went off. The lights went out.

Du Pré laughed. He finished his smoke and got back in his cruiser and drove on slowly, lights out, until he got to the fork in the road. The cruiser lumbered out into the main county road.

Benny Klein switched on his lights.

Du Pré switched on his.

The cars glared at each other.

Benny got out. He had a deputy with him, Bakula, a young rancher who needed a paycheck to keep his little spread going.

Du Pré put his cruiser in neutral and set the emergency brake and got out.

"Evenin', Gabriel," said Benny. He looked uncomfortable.

"Benny," said Du Pré.

"Uh," said Benny, "you mind tellin' me where you been?"

Du Pré jerked his head west. There was another road that went toward the headwaters of Cooper's Creek's east fork.

"There was some trouble out to the Eide place," said Benny.

"It's not the Eide place anymore," said Bakula.

"You got your gun?" said Benny, looking unhappily at Du Pré.

"Yah," said Du Pré. He took out his 9mm and he held it out. Bakula took it and he smelled the bore.

"Ain't been fired a while," said Bakula. He handed it back to Benny.

Benny relaxed.

"What the hell you doin' out in the country now?" said Benny.

"Birdwatching," said Du Pré. "It is hard to do at night. That is what cuts the experts from the amateurs."

Benny sighed.

"OK," he said, "ain't any of my bidness. You hear any gunfire."

"Yah," Du Pré said. "Some, an hour ago maybe. East. Pretty far off, you know."

Benny nodded.

"Well," he said, "I expect Bakula and me better go on, see what those yahoos want out at the ranch there."

"What happened?" said Du Pré.

"Somebody took some shots, beat the shit out of a watchman they say. Busted his nose bad."

Ah, them noses, Du Pré thought. Crack someone across the good part of the nose, break the bones, they can't see and it hurts bad, they don't think so good.

"Where?" said Du Pré. "He is watching the buildings there?"

"I dunno," said Benny. "Just some woman called. Said a watchman had called in, said he had been shot at and was gonna go take a look. They didn't hear nothing more."

Du Pré nodded.

"You need help?" he said.

Benny looked at him.

"Maybe tomorrow," he said. "If we find some tracks."

Du Pré nodded.

Benny and Bakula got in Benny's cruiser and they drove off toward the Host of Yahweh's ranch.

Du Pré drove back to Bart's, and he went in the house and to the room he had off the main living area. Bart had designed the house himself and Du Pré and Booger Tom had built most of it. Bart didn't like walls. The bedrooms and the bath were enclosed, but nothing else was. Du Pré stopped in front of a deliriously jumbled sculpture hanging on an outside wall. He wondered who the hell David Hockney was, again.

It was about four in the morning. Du Pré took a shower and he went to bed and tossed and turned and finally fell into a sort of sleep.

He dreamed of the badlands, of a man in armor with a crested helmet wandering thirsty, lost, sinking down upon his knees, crawling into a cave.

Du Pré woke up cranky. He smelled coffee.

He grabbed a towel and padded off to the shower and stood in it a long time, letting the hot water loosen the knots in his muscles.

He dried off and went back to his room and put on clean

clothes. He took the ones he had been wearing and went to the laundry room behind the bath and put them in the washer. Then he went out to find Bart sitting at the long counter drinking the thick black coffee he began each day with.

Du Pré poured himself a generous mugful and he slid up on a stool.

"Mornin'," said Bart. "If you hold your mouth right, that old bastard may join us for coffee. He's been feeling benevolent toward the peasants lately."

Du Pré nodded and then he sipped the hot black double-roast coffee.

All my life I drink coffee but I never drink coffee till I drink this.

Them Italians, they know some good things.

The door banged open and Booger Tom stomped in, rubbing his gnarled old hands, far too large for the man, grown to a life of hard work.

They look like tree roots, Du Pré thought.

"Any coffee for an old bastard?" said Booger Tom.

"Surely," said Bart, "you needn't address yourself so unkindly."

"Listen, pissant," said Booger Tom, "I know ya went to all kinda tony schools but you sound like ya got a poker up your ass. You gonna talk like that, hang your pinky out farther away from the cup, there."

Bart moved his little finger out. He wiggled it.

"More like it," said Booger Tom. He poured coffee for himself and dumped in a lot of sugar.

"That's bad for your teeth," said Bart.

Booger Tom slipped out his false teeth.

"You all right, boys?" he said, lisping. He looked intently at his store-boughts. He held his false teeth in his hand, fingers and thumb, and he clacked them together.

"Knew an old feller," said Booger Tom, "used to take out his choppers an' hol' 'em like this, and chop up his beefsteak or his bacon. It did cause comment in the better restaurants."

"It was *you*," said Bart. "Some ol' feller indeed."

Booger Tom put his teeth back in.

"Yes," he sighed. "This ol' gal was after me to marry her an' her folks come to take us out to dinner, and I had to do *somethin'* . . ."

Du Pré laughed silently.

"It work?" said Bart.

Booger Tom fingered a scar on his forehead.

"Yeah," he said. "She give me this with the pitcher of ice water. Said I was a hopeless, worthless son of a bitch."

Bart nodded.

"You tell her she was right?" said Bart.

"I did that," said Booger Tom. "Course, I'se a-layin' on the floor there in this puddle a icewater an' cubes. She said bye-bye with her right foot and busted three ribs."

"Women are dangerous," said Bart.

"Ya gotta keep movin'," said Booger Tom, "is all."

A big diesel roared out on the turnaround, and then the engine died to a popping.

They went to the door and looked out.

It was a stock hauler. The stock in the trailer was banging the walls ferociously. The trailer shook.

The driver got down and walked over.

"Sorry to trouble you," he said, "but I am lookin' for the Host a Yawow ranch or some damn thing. They said take the first left turn outta Toussaint."

"It's the second," said Bart, "and the second is a good six miles past the first. It goes off east there. The ranch is mostly east of the mountains."

The driver looked at the Wolf Mountains.

"Goddamn hippies," he said. "Well, I thank you."

Something heavy crashed against the aluminum side of the trailer. The metal bulged out and stayed there.

The driver threw his hat on the ground.

"God *damn*," he yelled. "I shoulda never agreed to haul these goddamned *buffalo.*"

The man got in the rig and made a long turn.

When the trailer passed close to the house, a bison shoved a horn right through the sheathing.

"Hope he makes it," said Booger Tom.

CHAPTER
10

"What happen out there?" said Madelaine. "I tol' you don't get angry."

"I am not angry," said Du Pré. "I did not kill the son of a bitch."

"We starting a war, Du Pré?"

Du Pré threw up his hands.

"Guy come after me, one of those four-wheelers, I am supposed to let him see me, I have shot his rifle to shit?"

"Son of a bitch," said Madelaine, "he is shooting the horses?"

Du Pré nodded.

"What these people want?" said Madelaine.

Du Pré shrugged.

The telephone rang. Du Pré looked at it.

"Don' answer that," he said. "I got a bad feeling."

Madelaine snorted.

She picked up the phone.

"Madelaine," she said. She listened.

"But how you dance with me you don't come here?" she said.

Shit, Du Pré thought, I know it is that damn Harvey before she pick it up.

"No, he is not uglier," said Madelaine. "He is about the same. So why you saying these bad things, my man?"

Madelaine listened for a moment. Then she roared with laughter.

"Your wife there, Harvey? Lemme talk, her," she said.

She grinned and handed the phone to Du Pré.

"Top of the morning," said Agent Harvey Wallace, a.k.a. Weasel Fat, Blackfeet, and FBI.

Du Pré grunted.

"You've met the Host of Yahweh?" said Harvey.

Du Pré grunted.

"Interesting folks," said Harvey. "Very big on purity, on worship, on hard work, on homeschooling. Turned a lot of lives around, they have."

Du Pré grunted.

"Clannish as the Mormons," said Harvey, "even clannish as the early Mormons. Very much like the early Mormons, matter of fact. You know about the Sons of Dan, the Danites?"

"Fuck," said Du Pré.

"Mind like a steel goat's," said Harvey. "Eight o'clock."

"Fuck," said Du Pré.

"It's boring talkin' with ya," said Harvey. "You wanna hear the story?"

"No," said Du Pré.

"You get to see the lovely agent Pidgeon," said Harvey.

"How many?" said Du Pré.

"Seven," said Harvey. "At eight o'clock last night, in places far apart, seven former members of the Host of Yahweh went to *meet* Yahweh. On the dot. Our friends there are punctual."

"How?" said Du Pré.

"Shot," said Harvey. "Very professional. Went to useful lengths. Used twenty-two's. Hollow points. Left the guns, which had no prints. All from a case of twelve stolen three years ago from an air cargo locker. Badda bip, badda boom."

"Where?" said Du Pré.

"Four in California, two in Oregon, one in New York. State, not city."

"Who were they?" said Du Pré.

"Former members," said Harvey. "Funny thing, not a one of them had said a bad word about the cult. None of them, far as we know now, seemed at all worried. They were working and living like plain folks. Now, usually, when anyone bails out of something like that, there is a little stink. A bitterness, the odd reference to evil. But not this time. They just left and now they are really gone."

Du Pré chewed his lip.

"OK," he said, "so you want me, do something."

"I hear you've already been doing *something*," said Harvey. "Maybe you could do a little legwork for me, maybe not so, well, *noticeable*."

Du Pré grunted.

"Agent Pidgeon is on her way," said Harvey.

"Why?" said Du Pré.

Harvey sighed.

"Because," he said carefully, "I know I can trust her."

"Ripper?" said Du Pré.

"Ripper is terrified of going to Montana," said Harvey. "What did you *do* to the poor boy? He is right here, pale and shaking."

"My little granddaughter, she says she is going, marry him," said Du Pré.

"Pallas?" said Harvey. "The sprout with the gone front teeth and the IQ of three hundred and fifty? Why, Ripper, what a lucky fellow . . . He's on the floor now, foaming at the mouth. He eats soap, you know."

Du Pré could hear Ripper hollering NONONONONONO-Noooooooooooaaaaaahh.

"Heh heh," said Harvey, "thankee kindly. Keeping Ripper in hand is, well, a handful, and by cracky you done give me the Club. I can't find words to thank you."

"FUCK FUCK FUCK FUCK FUCK fuuuuuuuuuuuuuckkkkk," said Ripper's croaky voice.

"He pissed his pants," said Harvey. "Well, I had Pallas after me, I'd soil myself, I suppose."

"What you want?" said Du Pré.

"Want?" said Harvey. "Why, how could you think such a thing of me? I merely called to discuss the *wedding plans!*"

Du Pré could hear Ripper moaning faintly and piteously.

"Fetch my shoe polishes," said Harvey. "Spit shine my Nu-Bucks here. You wanna go to Montana, Ripper? See your betrothed?"

Du Pré heard a door slam.

"He resigned again," said Harvey. "Just like that. Not to worry, it's the fourth time this week."

"It is Tuesday," said Du Pré.

"Short fuse, our Ripper," said Harvey. "What I *want*, see, is for you to find the killers, there, and truss them up, and tape the evidence to their foreheads, and give me a call."

Du Pré grunted.

"These are very dangerous people," said Harvey, "and I think that because until shortly after eight o'clock last night they had a most sterling reputation. Financial affairs in order. No complaints from members. High praise for the homeschooling program. Don't drink, don't smoke—you could join, there, Du Pré, think about it—and literally not one bad *rumor* . . . even their El Máximo seemed a good guy. Gary Carl Smith he was, before he became the White Priest. Wears spotless white robes, he does. Funny sandals, too, calls 'em *buskins.*"

"I need Ripper," said Du Pré.

"He won't like that," said Harvey.

"I get him now, you don't maybe drop him, an airplane later," said Du Pré.

"Still bitter about that, eh?" said Harvey. "I just send him out there to you by parachute and I thought it was funny, myself."

Du Pré grunted.

"He came back. He came back," said Harvey, "with my shoe polishes. No, those are *new* . . . address my brogans, lackey."

Du Pré heard a thud and a struggle going on.

"Ripper finally lost it?" said Madelaine. "I wondered about that."

Du Pré listened. Choking sounds.

Scritchings. Duct tape.

The phone was moved, tapped, and then Du Pré heard heavy breathing.

"This is Harvey's secretary," said Ripper. "He became indisposed. In fact, he has been delirious for two days. You musn't pay any attention to his ravings. He is unwell."

"Pidgeon is coming," said Du Pré. "You come, too."

"Ahhhh," Ripper whined. "I can't. I just can't. Out there, past Chicago, there be monsters. How is the little monster, anyway?"

"Ain't changed her mind," said Du Pré.

"The kid is what, now, ten?"

"Nearly eleven," said Du Pré.

"She terrifies me," said Ripper.

"Yah," said Du Pré.

"I will come on one condition," said Ripper. "You send her to some far place. Siberia would be good. Antarctica. I'd settle for Afghanistan."

"Cut the crap," said Du Pré. "We sit on her, you are such a wimp."

"You sit on her, you'll be a eunuch," said Ripper. "Harvey, just relax, willya. And I'm told it comes off with enough lighter fluid and sandpaper."

"You and Pidgeon," said Du Pré.

"Shit," said Ripper. "Shit."

"You, watch Pidgeon," said Du Pré.

Pidgeon was flat hands down the most beautiful woman that Du Pré had ever seen. Anyone else had, either. She was a red-bone. French, English, black, Cherokee, and what-all.

"I could do that," said Ripper.

"Let Harvey go home now," said Du Pré, "and wash off the shoe polish."

CHAPTER

11

Pidgeon and Ripper and Du Pré stood on a rock at the east end of the Wolf Mountains. Du Pré had set up his spotting scope, and through it they could clearly see what was going on in the Host of Yahweh compound.

Five stock haulers were there, unloading more buffalo. There were about a thousand animals in a huge pasture. Du Pré guessed that the grass there would last another week at most. Far out on the ranch's borders fencing crews were putting up miles of heavy four-strand fencing.

A horsefly buzzed lazily up and sat on Pidgeon's bare and lovely shoulder. She whacked it with her open hand and wrinkled her nose at the mess in her palm.

"Part of the Great Chain of Being, there," said Ripper, "and you just wipe the poor bastard out. What if it was a real rare and endangered kind of horsefly?"

"If the last goddamned Siberian tiger was licking his chops

in front of me," said Pidgeon, "I'd blow his ass away, too. Things don't have enough good sense to leave me alone, fuck 'em."

"Nice spread they got there," said Ripper. "Wonder how many of the killers are down there right now? Just worshiping away there."

Du Pré sighed. He put his eye to the spotting scope and stared. One of the men he had seen on the night that the Eide ranch burned was standing talking to a white-haired woman. They laughed and hugged and went off in different directions.

"Fucking Harvey," said Pidgeon, "I am supposed to be home with my computers. Cactus. I hate fucking cactus. Bugs."

"So?" said Ripper. "Since when did Harvey pay any attention to our whining? Since never. He's a sadist. Likes it, too."

"They generally do," said Pidgeon. "By the way, the killers were all women."

Ripper looked at her for a moment.

"Makes sense," he said.

"The victims were all men," said Pidgeon. "Dumb bastards."

"How you know that?" said Du Pré.

"Well," said Pidgeon, "we got the reports, the cops interviewed anyone'd stand still long enough, and, all these people were living in good apartments, families, like that, and no one saw anything unusual. That's what's unusual, that they saw nothing unusual. Women are less likely to attract attention. Maybe they are carrying a baby on a packboard. Or delivering some flowers. And the other funny thing was, all the victims were in the parking areas, about to go somewhere. At exactly eight o'clock. That means something, I dunno what."

"So?" said Ripper. "Host of Yahweh, very punctilious, I have heard."

"Yes," said Pidgeon, "they are. Well, it's nice to look at the buffalo roamin' and all but we aren't gonna see dick down there."

She was wearing chinos, low hiking boots, and a sleeveless

silk blouse, bright blazing blue. Her dark red hair flashed crimson lights and her deep green eyes glowed.

The 9mm Glock on her belt looked a bit out of place.

"Well," said Ripper, "I did want to see it."

"Harvey said the White Priest was on his way here. He was visiting congregations when the seven were killed. Should be along, soon," said Pidgeon.

"We don't got enough for a search warrant," said Ripper, "or a wiretap or a damn thing. Let's just shoot 'em all."

"I want some iced tea," said Pidgeon, "and it would be all right with me if you just left Ripper here with the spyglass. Let him look on a while."

"Awww," said Ripper, "you wound me."

"Yeah," said Pidgeon. "I will, that."

She began to walk back down the path toward Du Pré's old cruiser. Her perfect hips swayed perfectly. Her grace was equal to her beauty.

"Harvey thought I might join the Host, there," said Ripper, "but I personally don't think it'd work."

Du Pré looked at him.

Ripper crooked a finger. He bent to the eyepiece and he moved the spotting scope a little.

"Take a look," he said, "the doorway there."

Du Pré bent and squinted.

Du Pré stared.

Then he saw it.

Back in the dark there was a huge lens, and it was pointed directly at Du Pré.

"Bet that lens, it has a camera behind it," said Ripper. "Film in that camera, too, I bet."

Du Pré grunted.

"And," said Ripper, "I . . ." He bent to the eyepiece again. He moved the spotting scope.

Du Pré looked through it. A man was wiring up some small black boxes that were fastened chest high on fenceposts.

"Motion detectors," said Ripper. "Bet they got other stuff, too. The things that you can buy these days, mail order."

Du Pré stood up.

"Until there's a chink in the wall," said Ripper, "we're fucked. So I think I will just go on back to good old Washington, D.C."

Du Pré lifted the heavy spotting scope and he folded the legs up and snapped them into the holders along the tube. Then he slid the scope into the leather case and put the strap over his shoulder.

They walked down the path to the cruiser.

Pidgeon was standing by an open door. She was using it for a rest. Her Glock was pointing at something.

"Did you read 'em their rights?" said Ripper.

"A rattlesnake," said Pidgeon, "has no rights at all. God, I hate snakes."

Du Pré looked where her gun was pointing. A rattler was sunning on a rock. It was all of a foot long.

"Leave him," said Du Pré. "He will not bother you."

"I hate wildlife," said Pidgeon. "I hate all of 'em."

"We're gonna get you iced tea," said Ripper.

Pidgeon pulled her gun up. She popped the round out of the chamber and she put it back in the clip and she put the gun back in its holster.

She got in the backseat.

"I could ride back there," said Ripper.

"You see *The Godfather*?" said Pidgeon.

"Yes," said Ripper, "I did." He climbed into the backseat.

Du Pré put the spotting scope in the trunk. He drove down the dirt track and stopped and he went and got his .270 from the cleft in the rock. The 9mm was in the case. He put the rifle and pistol in the aluminum case with the foam points.

He got back in the car.

"Hiding guns?" said Ripper. "Waiting for the black helicopters, the forces of the Evil Government! We are here! I need to kick down a door."

Pidgeon looked out of the window.

Du Pré drove fast back to Toussaint. Madelaine was behind the bar, beading. She had on the ridiculous glasses that Du Pré had fashioned for her. She smiled when the three came in.

"Jesus," said Pidgeon, "I haven't seen anything that tasteful since Gianni Versace got himself shot."

Madelaine went on beading while Du Pré got sodas for the two FBI agents. He made whiskey and water for himself.

It was getting warm outside.

Du Pré heard gravel crunch under tires, but the engine noise wasn't there. Some new car with a good muffler.

He sipped his drink.

The door opened and a young woman came in, dressed in the long gray dress of the Host of Yahweh. She had a pretty, round face, and she wore the white bonnet the women favored.

"Do you have water?" she said.

"Sure," said Madelaine. She put down her beading.

She filled a big glass with ice.

"Oh, no," said the young woman. "I meant bottled water. Do you have any? Perrier or Poland Spring?"

Madelaine shook her head.

"*Nothing*?" said the young woman.

"Not many people come here," said Madelaine, "to drink the water."

The young woman hesitated.

"Thank you," she said. She went back out.

Du Pré went to the door and he opened it.

An incredibly long car was pulling out of the lot, a white car.

The windows were black.

"I do believe that is the White Priest," said Ripper.

Du Pré nodded. It was getting hot out, so he shut the door.

CHAPTER
12

"She is real pretty," said Pallas. She looked at Pidgeon.

"What's it to ya?" said Pidgeon.

Pallas went to the stool next to Agent Pidgeon and climbed up on it and put her little hands out.

"One," said Pallas, "is that I am marrying Ripper in six years. He's a guy, so, well . . . I can't blame him, I guess, but . . ."

"You think Ripper and I have a thing going?" said Pidgeon.

"Could," said Pallas.

"I don't want to belittle your taste in men," said Pidgeon, "but Ripper there, well, he doesn't exactly light my fire."

"You think he's ugly?" said Pallas.

"Nope," said Pidgeon.

"Stupid?" said Pallas.

"Nope," said Pidgeon.

"What's wrong with him?" said Pallas.

"Tell you what," said Pidgeon. "Marry his sorry ass and find out."

"Well-mannered people," said Ripper, "do not discuss others who are in the same room."

Pidgeon and Pallas looked at Ripper.

Ripper threw up his hands and went out the front door.

"Smart man," said Susan Klein. She made herself a drink and came down to Pidgeon and Pallas.

Pidgeon bent over close to Pallas.

"Actually," she whispered, "he's a great guy. Rare guy. We just have this way of working together."

"Why don't you like him?" said Pallas.

"I love this other guy," said Pidgeon, "but he doesn't even notice me."

"Doesn't notice *you*?" said Pallas. "He is dead, maybe?"

Pidgeon sighed.

"What can I tell ya?" she said.

"Who?" said Pallas.

Pidgeon squirmed.

"Um, I'd rather not," she said.

"OK," said Pallas, "I figure it out, though. I am good at figuring stuff out."

"I'd rather you didn't," said Pidgeon.

"You aren't very happy," said Pallas.

Pidgeon sighed.

"Pallas," she said, "you're picking on me."

"Yeah," said Pallas, "I am. I . . . maybe I am jealous. You are older. You are very beautiful. If I was you I could marry Ripper right now."

"Give it time," said Pidgeon.

"Easy for you to say," said Pallas.

Pidgeon sighed again.

"How 'bout a pop?" said Susan Klein.

Pallas nodded.

"OK," she said. "I am sorry. I got to pick on my brothers, sisters, all the time. Stay alive, you know."

Pidgeon nodded.

Madelaine came in the front door.

"Ripper is on his knees in the parking lot," said Madelaine. "He is calling on God for deliverance."

"Ripper is fond of cheap dramatics," said Pidgeon.

"What you doin' in here?" said Madelaine, looking hard at Pallas.

"I had talk to her 'bout Ripper," said Pallas.

"Uh-huh," said Madelaine. "You threaten, kill her?"

"No," said Pallas, "I was just explaining."

"Uh-huh," said Madelaine. She came up and got on the stool beside Pidgeon.

Pallas tried to be very small so that Madelaine would forget she was in the saloon where she wasn't supposed to be.

"Pallas goin' to marry Ripper," said Madelaine.

Pidgeon nodded.

"I expect she will," she said.

"Ripper, him, he think it is a joke," said Madelaine.

"Ripper is so smart about some things and so damn dumb about others," said Pidgeon. "Typical guy."

"Got two heads, think with the little one," said Pallas.

"That is enough," snapped Madelaine.

"Wherever did you hear *that*?" said Pidgeon.

"From me," said Madelaine. "She is not, say them things, company."

Pidgeon snorted.

"She is sad," said Pallas. "She is in love, this guy, he don't know she is alive."

Madelaine looked at Pidgeon.

"You like it he don't know?" she said.

Pidgeon nodded vigorously.

"See?" said Madelaine, looking at Pallas. "It is not so simple."

"It is not so complicated, either," said Pallas. "Get your head out of your ass it isn't anyway."

Madelaine sighed. Susan Klein brought her a glass of pink fizzy wine.

"We try," she said, "raise her right and all. She is born, this. First thing she say, the doctor picks her up she comes out. 'Who the fuck are you?' "

Pidgeon laughed.

"Well," said Pallas, "maybe I better go and see how Ripper is doing."

"Sight of you," said Madelaine, "calm him right down. Yep. Good of you, very Christian, go to help make poor Ripper feel better."

"Silly fucker," said Pallas. "He oughta go fishing or something." She finished her pop and she ran out.

Phrases of Ripper's address to the Lord God on High wafted in and were cut off when the door closed.

"Quite a kid," said Pidgeon.

"That one is never a kid," said Madelaine. "I think, maybe she is older than I am. Maybe who she marry oughta be Benetsee."

Susan Klein roared with laughter.

So did Pidgeon.

The door opened again and a woman came in, wearing the long gray dress of the Host of Yahweh. She had a rolled sheet of paper in her hand. She walked up to the bar.

"Could I possibly put this up?" she said. "We are having a barbecue Sunday afternoon, and wish to invite anyone who would like to come. There will be barbecued buffalo and trimmings, pop, beer, and we hoped we might hire Mr. Du Pré and his band to play."

"Him can't," said Madelaine, "other musicians are at Turtle Mountain, they be here, maybe two weeks."

"Too bad," said the woman. "But we have some pretty good

musicians, too. You are all invited, of course. So may I put this up?"

"Sure," said Susan Klein. She pointed to the big corkboard by the door where messages and advertisements were posted.

The woman put up the poster, an expensive four-color print.

Madelaine went over to look at it.

"They have that printed just for this," she said. "Cost some money, that."

"We have been racking our brains trying to find an excuse to get in there," said Pidgeon. "And look at this."

"Won't do you much good," said Susan Klein.

Pidgeon shrugged.

Du Pré came in. He left the door open for a moment.

"Ripper he is praying for lightning," said Du Pré, "strike Pallas."

"What is Pallas doing?" said Madelaine.

"Laughing at Ripper," said Du Pré, "the dumb shit."

"What you doing, Du Pré?" said Madelaine.

Du Pré shrugged and he let the door close.

"I am being thirsty," he said.

Susan Klein got a tall glass and she made a ditch for Du Pré.

"You see the woman who was just in here?" said Madelaine.

"Yah," said Du Pré, "invite everybody, a barbecue, the Eide place."

"She want you to play there," said Madelaine.

Du Pré shook his head.

"They ask you again," said Madelaine.

"They ask a lot I still shake my head," said Du Pré.

"So the White Priest is here," said Pidgeon, "and the carnival begins."

She walked over to the poster and looked at it carefully.

"Anybody can come in a costume," said Pidgeon. "A hundred dollar prize for the best one."

"Ripper win that," said Du Pré.

Dress up, the Mad Hatter, when we raid that dope operation. Jesus.

Pidgeon came back to her stool. Susan Klein patted her hand.

"Room all right, dear?" she said. There were two trailers out back of the saloon that each had three rooms.

"Jes' a little hole," said Pidgeon. "Jes' a little hole and it all pours through . . ." She stood up and went out the back door.

"What the hell is she talking about?" said Susan Klein.

"Seven murder cases and her love life," said Madelaine.

CHAPTER 13

"They were desperate," said Bart's lawyer Foote, "and there was a mailing which came, offering a low rate on a large loan. It seemed to be a legitimate offer, so the Eides applied and the loan was granted. Then the cattle business sank, hard, and there they were. The loan was cheap, all right, but the gamble was that beef would rise a little. It couldn't be rescheduled. So the Host of Yahweh foreclosed on it and that was that."

"They send this one thing just to the Eides?" said Du Pré.

"So far," said Foote. "I would expect that they did offer cheap money to a few other places."

"Bastards," said Du Pré.

"They were too proud to approach Bart," said Foote.

Du Pré sighed.

To some, Bart was just another rich newcomer, though the Fascellis had owned their ranch now for over forty years.

"It's very hard to get information," said Foote. "The members won't talk. There are very few apostates, and after the massacre no one in their right mind would say anything."

"Who is this White Priest?" said Du Pré.

"Seems to be your garden-run sociopath and manic-depressive," said Foote. "Very smart. Something is going on with the Host, but nobody can figure out what. They have a lot of legitimate businesses, a hell of a lot of money, and they haven't been stupid enough to try and buy automatic weapons from an FBI agent, at least not yet. They probably will. The White Priest declares that there will be spaceships coming to carry the faithful away, just before the world ends in fire and war. Think that, you need a few machine guns."

"Flying saucers?" said Du Pré.

"Last I read," said Foote, "over three million Americans recall having been abducted by aliens. Makes you believe in democracy, yes?"

Du Pré laughed.

"Why buffalo?" said Du Pré.

"Buffalo are well thought of," said Foote, "like wolves and harp seals. We live in a time of sentiment, unfortunately much like that of Germany circa 1936."

"Nazis?" said Du Pré.

"Hitler was a fascist," said Foote, "and fascists don't like dirt, sloppiness, tardiness, loud noises, smells, and other evidences of wrong thinking. If some good soul had shot Adolf in 1936, he would be Saint Adolf of the Ecology today. Loved wildlife, Hitler did. His SS had great reverence for all life, save inconvenient humans."

Du Pré snorted.

"We'll talk again. Be careful. Unlike most of these cults, there are some competent people in the Host."

Foote said goodbye and he was gone. Du Pré folded up the cell phone and he handed it back to Bart.

"I half expected a call from the cult," said Bart, "but it seems they have their own excavators. They are utterly self-contained.

Easier now with the Internet. They ship in their foodstuffs, clothing, necessaries. Other than deliveries of fuel and power they don't spend a nickel locally. They don't hire local craftsmen. They barely leave the ranch. And they offer a free barbecue to the neighbors. *That* should be interesting."

Du Pré nodded.

Pidgeon came in the back door of the saloon. It was a warm day and she had on shorts and a halter. Two cowboys at a table in the corner stared at her, mouths open.

"I have some stuff," said Pidgeon. She went back out.

The cowboys looked at each other and they shook their heads.

Du Pré slid off the stool and he went out the back door to the double room Pidgeon had in the larger of the two trailers. She had set up an office. There was a fair-sized telephone bank and some other electronic equipment Du Pré did not recognize and didn't care to know about, either.

There were seven color photographs printed on 8½ × 11 sheets of paper tacked to a corkboard. The photographs were grainy, blowups of those taken for driver's licenses.

All men, all in their mid-thirties, all with neat haircuts and open, level gazes, and all dead at the same instant though they were hundreds of miles apart.

"My clients there," said Pidgeon, "pretty ordinary joes, every one. None of them were in the military. They went to middling schools and got degrees in ordinary disciplines. All having to do with the computer. Computer science, advertising, marketing, and information retrieval. That's what librarians are today. Information retrieval specialists."

Du Pré looked at the faces. They were meaningless.

"Other'n they all got killed the same moment," said Pidgeon, "neither I nor my alchemies can spot any pattern. Four were married and divorced before they joined the Host, three divorced after they joined the Host, not a one of them ever got busted for anything 'cept overtime parking. Dull, honest citizens, other'n believing spaceships were coming and what-all else the Host thinks, they were all duller than network TV. Why somebody thought they all had to be killed is mysterious. These guys would be invisible in a gray room."

Du Pré stared at the photographs.

"Maybe I have copies of these?" he said.

Pidgeon looked at him.

"Sure," she said. "Take about five minutes." She did something on a keyboard and noises began. A printer pushed out a sheet of paper.

"I was going to take these to Benetsee," said Pidgeon. "We need a little magic."

Du Pré laughed.

Pidgeon waited while the photographs came out of the slot. She put them in a manila envelope and handed it to Du Pré.

"Where is that Ripper?" said Du Pré.

"In a phone company truck," said Pidgeon, "hanging off a pole out at the Host Ranch. Looking around. Won't amount to shit, but at least I don't have to listen to his godawful jokes."

"They are pretty bad," said Du Pré.

Ripper loved puns, the more wretched the better.

"Couple agents from out Butte office are coming to talk to the White Priest," said Pidgeon, "ask questions about the late lamented. This is the first and only spot of trouble the Host of Yahweh has ever had. It is odd as hell. Other'n the spaceships and the White Priest, there isn't anything even especially weird about them."

"Give Harvey my best," said Du Pré.

"I'd like to give Harvey a whack over the head with a chair," said Pidgeon. "I coulda done this at home, damn it." She punched savagely at her keyboard.

Du Pré took the envelope and went out.

The day was bright and there were only a few puffy clouds high up. The sun was very warm on his back. He wore an old shirt with the sleeves ripped off at the shoulder seams. The air felt good.

Du Pré yawned.

Funny dreams last night, but they are not funny. Make no sense. Only times my dreams make sense I go to Benetsee's, but those are not dreams.

Du Pré shrugged and went in the back door of the Toussaint Bar. The cowboys were still at the table in the corner, still looking poleaxed. Madelaine was behind the bar. She was still wearing the ridiculous rhinestone glasses.

She was staring at her beadwork.

Du Pré leaned over the bar. He snatched the godawful glasses and threw them on the floor and stomped on them. Blue rhinestone beads crunched and plastic shattered. He twisted his bootheel.

Du Pré went and got the broom and dustpan and swept up the pieces and took them to the cold woodstove and threw them in. He put the broom and dustpan back.

He sat back down on the barstool.

Madelaine had on another pair of glasses, the spare set of plain fake tortoiseshell Du Pré had bought in Cooper.

"I win five dollars," said Madelaine. "I know you do that, I say today. That Susan, she say, no, tomorrow. So we bet."

"You know me pret' good," said Du Pré.

Madelaine looked up and she smiled.

"You know me pret' good, too," she said. She put down her beadwork and glasses. She came round the bar and put her arms around Du Pré and kissed him.

The cowboys at the table cheered.

Madelaine turned and bowed.

Du Pré laughed.

Madelaine went back to her stool behind the bar.

Du Pré looked at the floor. He saw a piece of blue bead he had missed.

But when he bent over to pick it up, he couldn't see it.

CHAPTER
14

Du Pré drove his old cruiser through the front gate of the Host ranch, and down the recently graded road to the main compound. There were perhaps forty vehicles parked on a lot marked out with lines of white powder. Some were Host of Yahweh vans and some were pickups and cars owned by local people.

One of the huge metal buildings had its front doors slid open, and lights shone inside.

"Wonder what they got?" said Madelaine.

They got out. Ripper and Pidgeon had been sitting in the backseat, silently. They got out, too.

"Jacqueline and Raymond and the kids be along," said Madelaine.

The four of them walked toward the big metal building. There were rain clouds off to the west. A huge area down in a meadow had been made over into a softball field and a soccer field and there was an elaborate playground, with slides and jungle gyms and swings and sandboxes.

Inside the barn, tables had been set up and hundreds of folding chairs. There was a bandstand and many booths with carnival games. Tossing rings, shooting air guns at spinning targets, throwing balls at stacks of fake bottles. There were shelves of prizes, mostly stuffed animals. Some of the booths sold preserves and baked goods and clothing.

The members of the Host of Yahweh were bustling around, hanging the last of the bunting and arranging the last few things, forgotten till that moment.

"Don't look too dangerous," said Madelaine.

Du Pré nodded.

The rear door of the metal barn was open, too, and scents of cooking meat and barbecue sauce blew through the barn.

There was a cotton candy machine in one corner, and some kids in line waiting to get really sticky.

Ripper and Pidgeon split up and they sauntered around the booths.

Madelaine stopped at one of the shooting galleries. She began to dig in her purse for some money.

"It's free," said the young man in the old-blood-colored shirt.

Madelaine shrugged and she picked up one of the little air rifles and she aimed it at a target swinging on a stand. She pulled the trigger and the pellet rang on the target. The center red circle fell out of the thing and on to a bell.

"Top shelf," said the young man. "Anything you want."

Madelaine regarded the large stuffed bunnies and monkeys and bears.

"That one," she said, pointing to a big brown rabbit.

She handed her prize to Du Pré.

"Look good on you," she said, standing back.

Du Pré looked at the big rabbit.

"I put it in the car," he said.

I am not, me, walking around this thing.

"I look around," said Madelaine.

Du Pré heard a mob of happy little voices coming.

"They are here," he said, looking toward the front door.

Jacqueline's herd of children burst out of the sunlight, laughing and shoving each other. Raymond and Jacqueline came along behind, each carrying a toddler who was too slow to keep up.

Du Pré put the rabbit up to his face, and he walked past the kids who were looking around in wonder. He went to the cruiser and opened the back door and put the huge rabbit on top of the cooler. He fished his flask from under the seat and he had some whiskey and rolled a smoke. He lit it and shut the car door.

"Mr. Du Pré?" said a woman's voice, behind him.

Du Pré turned around.

It was the young woman who had brought the poster to the saloon a few days before.

"If you aren't busy," she said, "someone would like to meet you and speak to you for a moment."

Du Pré nodded.

The woman turned and walked away, and Du Pré followed. She came to a door in the end of one of the prefab houses and opened it. Du Pré dropped his cigarette on the ground and snuffed it with his bootheel. He went in and the woman followed him, shutting the door.

There were two men in the room, both dressed in Host costume. One was the blond man Du Pré had seen here the night the ranch buildings burned.

The other man had brown hair. It was hard to make out his face, because he had a wide white bandage crossing the bridge of his nose and his eyes were bruised.

"Hello again," said the bandaged man.

"You haven't met Roger," said the blond man, "at least not to shake hands. I am Tate."

Du Pré nodded.

"We were told that the wild horses were pests and we could shoot them without anyone caring," said Roger. "Since we are fencing off their pasture and water, and they would then have to leave, where another rancher would shoot them, and, by the bye, be angry with us for sending vermin his way, we thought to kill them. You object."

Du Pré nodded.

Roger looked at Tate.

"This is our land," said Tate, "and we will obey the laws. But we can hardly leave that end of the ranch unfenced. Buffalo aren't cattle."

Du Pré looked at Roger.

"Fence it off," he said. "That is fair. Them horses, been there a long time. There are grullas in that bunch."

Tate and Roger looked at him.

"Old horses," said Du Pré. "Maybe close to what the wild horses were, people caught, thousands of years ago."

"Very well," said Tate.

"People hunt them for pet food," said Roger.

Du Pré shook his head.

"Not here," he said.

Roger stood up. He put out his hand.

"Apologies," he said.

"Things rightly solved?" said a rich deep voice behind Du Pré.

Du Pré turned.

A man stood there, in a long white robe. The rope around his waist was white. There was a crucifix and beads on the rope, all white. He had a single ring on the middle finger of his right hand, a white stone in a white setting.

"I am the White Priest," said the man.

Du Pré nodded.

"We assumed when we came here that we would offend," said the White Priest. "We are odd, and keep to ourselves. We do that because we are all at risk, Mr. Du Pré, for all of us, myself included, had other lives which nearly killed us. Drugs, booze, whatever. So we stay close to one another. Now we have come to a remote place. We wish to live in peace and harmony with our neighbors. We will not proselytize. We will not attempt to take over the school board, or the County Commission. But however well-intentioned we may be, we will offend. Could we perhaps hire you as a consultant? We would pay any reasonable fee."

Du Pré looked at the three men.

"Who said, shoot the horses?" he said.

"I did," said Tate. "We have the damned brumbies in Nevada, and they are a pain in the ass. I am a ranch kid, Mr. Du Pré. Different country but pretty much the same."

"You don't got to pay me," said Du Pré, "and it don't matter, you call me, someone else. Call somebody. You are fencing your land off, no problem, you are not in a place it is wrong to do that. There are some. Fence off them badlands, OK, them horses go round the Wolfs, the Trapper Springs. They do that anyway."

"My apologies," said Tate.

"Your nose there, I am sorry," said Du Pré, looking at Roger. Roger shrugged.

"I ain't that pretty to begin with," he said.

"Great," said the White Priest. "Now, I suppose that everyone thinks we killed the seven former members who were shot, at precisely eight P.M. on the same day. We did not. The FBI is welcome to look at all of our records, interview whomever they wish."

Du Pré nodded.

"Anyone may leave here any time they wish to," said the White Priest. "It would hardly work if we had to chain people, now would it? We are a collective. But one takes no oath when they join, and suffers no consequences when leaving. I am telling you the simple truth, Mr. Du Pré."

Du Pré nodded.

"I go, my family," he said. He turned and went past the White Priest and out the door into the sunlight.

The huge carcasses were turning on spits over low fires and a pair of cooks were slathering on barbecue sauce with brooms.

It smelled very good.

CHAPTER
15

The band did a fair imitation of Irish folk music. Guitar, fiddle, hand drum, flute, and close harmonies. The musicians were young and fresh-faced and earnest.

"Them, want to be liked," said Madelaine. She put another piece of barbecued buffalo in her mouth and chewed.

Du Pré grunted.

"Working at it very hard," said Madelaine. "You see, that woman there with the cold drinks?"

Du Pré looked toward where Madelaine had nodded. The woman was dressed in the long gray dress and bonnet and plain wire-rim glasses that were the uniform of Host women.

"Yah," said Du Pré.

"She limp a little. She is the one maybe the skunk bit, Benetsee's?"

Du Pré looked at her. She didn't look familiar, but then she had been against the light of the sun if it was the woman that the skunk had bitten that day at the old man's cabin.

"Maybe," said Du Pré. "I don't see her so good."

Some Host children ran past, dressed in miniature outfits that echoed the grownups'. They were laughing and chaffing like any other kids.

"You are thinking, Du Pré," said Madelaine, "that is a good thing but maybe you don't think in one place too long, eh?"

Du Pré laughed.

"Yah," he said.

"If this is fake," said Madelaine, "there will be something don't fit. Lies got to be made up and the truth just happens."

Du Pré laughed. They walked outside and looked at the Wolf Mountains to the west. They had clouds hanging right over the highest peaks.

"Early for the circle rains," said Madelaine.

"Yah," said Du Pré.

Clouds formed above the peaks by day as the sun evaporated moisture, and then at night the clouds fell as dew. In the early morning the sky would be clear, and then clouds would build and gather as the day went on. It meant there was no wind. No rain coming, either.

A tan government sedan pulled into the lot where the cars and vans and pickup trucks of the guests were parked.

A man and a woman in gray suits got out. They looked round for a moment, and then Tate came out of the building where Du Pré had spoken with him, the man with the broken nose, and the White Priest. Tate trotted up to the two agents and led them back to the building and through the door Du Pré had gone in a couple of hours before.

"That Ripper and Pidgeon they are undercover," said Madelaine. "Them two look like bugs on a bedsheet."

Du Pré laughed.

"This White Priest," said Du Pré, "him say they don't want no trouble, they don't got anything to do with the murders."

"You believe him?" said Madelaine.

"No," said Du Pré, "don't not believe him, either. They say they will call me, they are going to do something."

"Like shoot the horses?" said Madelaine.

Du Pré nodded.

"They know a lot," said Madelaine, " 'bout raising buffalo, which is not like cattle. Where they find that all out?"

"Books," said Du Pré.

Madelaine laughed.

"Dessert," she said. "Me, I want some."

They went back in the big metal barn and found a booth that served ice cream. Madelaine had two scoops of strawberry. Du Pré had some whiskey from his pocket flask.

Raymond and Jacqueline and their herd were gathering at the far end of the building. Jacqueline said something forcefully. The children cast their eyes down and then the family began to walk out toward the parked van that they had come in. When they got close Pallas scooted out from the tangle and she ran up to Du Pré and Madelaine.

"You maybe take me back. I want to stay," she said. She narrowed her eyes.

"*Non,*" said Madelaine. "You go on with your people."

Pallas knew better than to argue with a *non.*

"Good time," said Raymond, when he got close. He was carrying a small child and a large stuffed monkey.

"We got tired kids getting cranky," said Madelaine.

"I am not tired," said Pallas.

"You," said Jacqueline, "you maybe take a nap when we get home, you want to or not."

Pallas dug her toe in the dirt.

"Shit," she said.

"You are being spoiled," said Raymond. "You stop now. Eh?"

Pallas nodded.

"We see you later maybe," said Jacqueline. They took their tired herd off to the big dark green van and everybody got in and Raymond started it and they drove off.

Du Pré and Madelaine watched them go. Du Pré rolled a cigarette and lit it and Madelaine took her long drag. He smoked the rest of it and then he put it out on the ground and they wandered back into the big metal building.

Pidgeon was shooting at the targets in the little gallery booth. Du Pré and Madelaine walked up to her. She was aiming very deliberately and taking her time and missing.

She took the little air rifle down from her shoulder.

"There's a trick to this," she said, looking at them.

"Sights are set off," said Du Pré. "Use the barrel."

"Oh," said Pidgeon.

The young man in the booth was staring at her and trying hard not to seem to be staring at her.

Pidgeon stuck the rifle to her shoulder and she pulled the trigger and the bull's-eye fell out. It went *pank* on the metal pan.

"Top shelf," said the young man. His voice was a croak. Pidgeon was making his mouth dry.

"I'll take the bear," said Pidgeon. "The big pink one there."

The young man handed her prize to her.

Pidgeon held the fat fluffy thing out at arm's length.

"A thing of beauty is a joy forever," she said.

"Amen," said the man in the booth, and then he flushed red.

Pidgeon ignored him. She tucked the big pink bear under her arm and sauntered toward the door that led out to the parked cars.

Du Pré and Madelaine followed after her. She walked slowly and gracefully, head down, lost in thought.

She got to the cruiser and opened the back door, shoved the big pink bear in and shut the door.

"Could I have a smoke?" she said.

Du Pré rolled one and he held it out. Pidgeon stuck it in her lips and she held out her hand. Du Pré gave her his shepherd's lighter.

Pidgeon lit the cigarette and she inhaled deep.

"Ahhhhh," she said. "It's unhealthy and I like it."

Du Pré shrugged. He had never seen her smoke before.

"Charming," said Pidgeon. She nodded toward the carnival in the barn.

"They want to be liked," said Madelaine.

"Bunch of crap," said Pidgeon.

Madelaine shrugged.

"They hauled you off," said Pidgeon, looking at Du Pré.

Du Pré nodded.

"Nice barbecue," said Pidgeon, "nice booths, free shit, and about five percent of the county came."

"Most people are suspicious," said Madelaine.

"Dunno why," said Pidgeon. "Me, I am, too, even though I did get a nice big pink bear. I will send it to Harvey. With a note, says, well I am working hard and how are you?"

Du Pré saw two men walking toward the building that he had gone into hours before.

One of them was Ripper.

"You get the pitch," said Pidgeon. "You get the *ad*, Du Pré?"

"Guy with a busted nose tell me they will not shoot the wild horses," said Du Pré, "said they call me they don't know what to do."

Pidgeon nodded.

"Yeah," she said. "And you met the White Priest?"

"Yah," said Du Pré, "long hair, beard, sandals, all white, white robe and crucifix."

"What color hair?" said Pidgeon.

Du Pré shrugged.

"Brown," he said. "Little gray in it."

"Real nice voice the White Priest has," said Pidgeon.

Du Pré nodded.

Pidgeon dropped her cigarette.

"Wasn't him," she said.

CHAPTER 18

Pidgeon was listening intently to her cell phone.

"Screw you, Harvey," she said. "I quit. There isn't a thing for me to do here I cannot do at home. Go ahead, fire me. Have a good time. I will be in on the late plane from Cincinnati."

Pidgeon listened intently to her cell phone.

"Piss up a rope, Harvey," she said, "and then stand under it while it dries." She shut her cell phone.

"Harvey sends his love," said Pidgeon.

Du Pré nodded. He slowed down to eighty-five. There was a crossroads up ahead and the left was blind. A low hill hid the road.

"Poor Harvey," said Madelaine, "he tries so hard."

"What he's trying to do," said Pidgeon, "is get me to stay here so he doesn't have to come."

Du Pré snorted.

"I leave you the excellent Ripper," said Pidgeon. "That little monster might even get himself killed this time. Luck happens, you know."

Pidgeon was in the backseat of the cruiser with her big pink stuffed bear and her gear was piled under it and in the trunk. She was dressed in a tan twill suit, good to travel in.

"You be back," said Madelaine, "you be back." It wasn't a question.

"Du Pré," said Pidgeon, "you be real careful around these people. They are good. Man, are they good."

"Who is this White Priest?" said Du Pré.

"Gary Carl Smith," said Pidgeon. "Problem is, we don't know which one or if that *is* his name. Nobody we know knows what he looks like. Always in a costume, got his head wrapped in a scarf. Like Peter O'Toole in *Lawrence of Arabia*. Got some stand-ins. You met one of 'em."

They were past the crossroads so Du Pré got up to cruising speed.

"Ya know," said Pidgeon, "when I fly, I sorta like having wings on what I'm flyin' in. A quirk, but I got it. *You goddamn halfbreed son of a bitch, slow this motherfucker down!*"

Du Pré slowed to ninety.

"More," said Pidgeon.

Du Pré slowed to seventy.

"So," said Du Pré, "we don't know the White Priest is here even."

"Nope," said Pidgeon.

"Him kill those people, though."

"Well," said Pidgeon, "it seems damned likely, as there isn't another thread that connects. But there's always a possibility it *could* be somebody else who wanted to set them up. Could be the Russians, all we know. Osama Bin Laden. Aliens."

Du Pré sighed. He reached under the seat for his flask.

"Du Pré," said Madelaine, "that mean blond Highway Patrol

lady is up here some and she want, toss you in the can, weld it shut, you know."

Du Pré put the flask back.

"Which lady?" said Pidgeon.

"Officer Parker," said Madelaine. "She about bust Du Pré there but McPhie he come along, he say, you behave now, Du Pré. You get a license and you quit drinkin' so much, driving a hundred twenty."

"They have actual *police* out here?" said Pidgeon.

"Yah," said Du Pré, "give you ticket bad breath, goin' too fast, just like that Washington, D.C."

"Du Pré," said Pidgeon, "it is the law, you know. How fast are we going?" Pidgeon leaned over the seat.

Seventy.

They passed a Montana Highway Patrol car hiding in a cut a ranch road took off from.

Pidgeon looked back through the window.

"Ah-haaaaahhhhh," she said. "Here they come, lights a-blazin'."

Du Pré looked in the rearview mirror.

"What the fuck," he said. "I am obeying the speed limit."

He slowed and pulled off on the shoulder.

The Highway Patrol car stopped, lights flashing. The door of the car opened and Officer Parker got out. She was about five feet tall and blond. She wore big black mirrored glasses.

Du Pré rolled down his window.

Parker came up to it. She bent over and put her head in.

"You OK," she said.

"Yah," said Du Pré. "I am doing the damn speed limit, yes?"

"Yeah," said Parker, "you were, which worried the hell out of me. There's Du Pré I says to myself, and he musta been carjacked cause he is just driving the speed limit. Little under actually. You feel all right?"

"I am fine," said Du Pré.

"Well," said Officer Parker, "I just needed to know this lady in the back there wasn't holding a gun to the back of your head."

"No," said Du Pré.

"I am encouraged," said Officer Parker, "since there is hardly any reek of bourbon about you, too. You all right? Didn't take the cure or anything?"

Du Pré spread his hands.

"McPhie even told me that you got an actual driver's license," said Parker, "a real one, good now till 2007, one of those hundred dollar ones lasts eight whole years. Got your picture on it and everything."

Du Pré started digging for his wallet. He fished his license out and he handed it to Officer Parker.

"Son of a bitch," said Parker, "that lyin' sack of shit McPhie wasn't a lyin' sack of shit for once." She handed back the license.

"Well," said Officer Parker, "I will now let you go on your merry way and I will go back in my hole and wait for a miscreant to come along. It is my job and I love it . . . Whoa—" and she fell back and pulled out her gun.

"Outta the car, hands behind your head," she screamed.

She was pointing the gun at Pidgeon.

"No!" Du Pré roared. "She is FBI!"

Parker's eyes flicked from Du Pré to Madelaine to Pidgeon, who had her hands up.

"Special Agent Pidgeon Federal Bureau of Investigation," said Pidgeon, "I have ID."

"Du Pré?" said Parker.

"Yes," said Du Pré.

"I just saw the damn gun," said Parker.

Du Pré turned. Pidgeon had unbuttoned her jacket and the butt of her Glock showed, barely, above her right hip.

Parker breathed deeply and she raised her stainless steel automatic.

"Wheeyew," she said. "Gave me a start."

Pidgeon got out of the car. She held out her ID.

"It's fine," said Parker. "One of those misunderstandings."

Officer Parker walked back to her cruiser, got in, and turned it round and headed northeast.

Pidgeon watched her go.

"Jesus," she said. "How these things happen."

"Yah," said Du Pré, "I am driving slow and get us mostly killed."

Pidgeon's cell phone chirred.

"Grrrr," she said. She opened the thing.

"Listen asshole," she snarled, "I—"

She flushed.

"Yes, sir," she said. "I was perhaps a little rude there. . . ."

She listened some more.

"No, he's fine," said Pidgeon. "We just have this routine, you know. Yeah, I will. I'll be in tomorrow."

She shut the cell phone, got back in the car, and Du Pré drove on.

They came near to Billings and Du Pré took a back road that led them up on the Rims to the airport. He drove up to the short-term lot and they got out and all of them carried things into the Delta counter.

"We go now," said Du Pré. "You tell that Harvey hello for us, we see him here soon."

Pidgeon nodded. She and Madelaine hugged and she kissed Du Pré on the cheek.

"I am sure I'll get sent back, too," said Pidgeon.

"This is pret' bad," said Madelaine. She was looking at Pidgeon.

Pidgeon nodded.

"We go after criminals," she said. "Truth to tell, most of 'em don't have enough brains to scrape over a cracker. But a few do. I dunno what's goin' on with this cult, but it's not good."

Du Pré nodded.

"After that fuckup in Waco," said Pidgeon, "cults make us all very very nervous indeed."

CHAPTER

17

"I would dearly love to get in there," said Ripper. He was peering through Du Pré's spotting scope. He pulled his head away.

The scope was trained on the largest of the metal buildings. Unlike the others, it did not have huge sliding doors, only wide double-hinged ones. That aside, it was the same featureless cream metal siding as the others. The roof was a middling blue.

Du Pré grunted.

They were hidden in a copse of junipers, the lens of the scope sleeved so that the sun would not flash on it. They had been there since an hour before dawn.

"That," said Ripper, "is the most utilitarian cathedral I ever saw. Notre Dame for utter shitheads. Up, there they go."

He bent his head to the lens and he stared.

"They're filing in there," he said. "Sunday services I bet. You want to take a look?"

Du Pré nodded.

He looked through the lens. The sixty-power scope was trained on a set of double doors that people were filing through. There were four guards at the doors, young men in the dark-red billowing shirts of the Host. They stood, arms folded across their chests.

The people going into the building halted and were briefly inspected. Well-mannered children stood quietly by their parents.

A middle-aged couple and two teenagers stopped.

Du Pré stared through the lens.

Bud and Millie Eide.

Du Pré looked again, unbelieving.

"Christ," he said, standing up. "It is them Eide. They are members of this thing."

"The former owners?" said Ripper. "Well, now we know why they didn't call Bart."

"They come to the party we throw for them," said Du Pré, "and are all sad at leaving. We feel sorry for them."

"People," said Ripper. "Shit."

It took twenty minutes for all of the people streaming out of the prefabricated houses to file into the big metal building. The guards stood together for a moment, talking, and then they went inside and shut the doors.

"Well," said Ripper, "we got up in the morning too damn early but we know a little more than we did."

Du Pré rolled a smoke.

"This," he said, "it is not good."

He looked up at the golden eagles circling high above.

"Du Pré!" said Ripper. "Look!"

Du Pré followed Ripper's pointing finger.

A figure was moving near one of the prefab houses.

Du Pré sighted the spotting scope on the place. It took a moment but he finally found her.

A young woman with two small children was tying a pack on the back of a four-wheeler. She put the kids on and strapped them with bungee cords. Then she started the machine and she drove off to the north and east. She dashed down the road and when she came to the gate at the end of the huge pasture she got off and opened it and then she drove through and closed it and she went on.

"We got a runner," said Ripper. "We had better get after her. They'll be after her the moment that they know she's gone."

Du Pré tried to spot the woman but she had disappeared behind the rolling earth.

Then he saw her. She was driving up a steep track, toward the back fence.

Toward the *malpais*, the badlands.

"Can we drive there?" said Ripper.

Du Pré thought.

"We go round," he said. "There is a road high there"—he pointed to a faint line on the flanks of the Wolf Mountains—"we go to Hulme's place, borrow some horses, maybe some four-wheelers."

"All the same to you," said Ripper, "I'd like a four-wheeler."

Du Pré shrugged.

He slipped the spotting scope back in the case and he slung it on his shoulder. Ripper had the cooler and the light folding chairs.

They tossed the gear in the backseat of Du Pré's old cruiser. He started it and turned round and drove back along the track. When he turned right on the county road he speeded up. It was a good gravel road, good for seventy miles an hour.

Du Pré wound up a grade and he got to the road that ran along the flanks of the Wolf Mountains. It was a bad road and he had to slow to fifty. The cruiser leaped off steep drops and bottomed on its springs.

"Hail, Mary, fulla grace!" screamed Ripper. He was crossing himself.

"You are Episcopalian," shouted Du Pré over the crashes, roars, screeches, and thumps.

"I am Everything," screamed Ripper. "I am All."

Du Pré fishtailed up a wide spot in the road and shot down a flat straightaway. When they got to the end of the flat, the road dropped off the bench. The Hulme place was three miles away, in a little cut valley, in a grove of cottonwoods and firs.

Du Pré wound through the tight narrow road. He turned into the ranch track and accelerated, then braked when he got to the main house. He jumped out and ran toward the door.

Mrs. Hulme came out, drying her hands on a dishtowel.

"Mr. Du Pré!" she said, smiling. "Whatever is the matter?"

"There is some trouble," said Du Pré. "We need horses, or maybe them four-wheelers, you got any."

Mrs. Hulme dropped the towel on the porch. She motioned for Du Pré to follow and led him to a low machine shed and pulled open one of the wide sliding doors.

Three four-wheel ORVs sat there.

Mrs. Hulme opened a gas tank. She shook her head and put the cap back on, then got on the ORV and started it and ran it out to the gasoline tank, set up on its timber frame. She filled the tank.

Du Pré brought another one and she filled that, too, and then she lifted a five-gallon plastic gas can and filled it. She found a blue one and filled that.

"You'll need water," said Mrs. Hulme.

She drove the ORV to the cruiser and Du Pré followed with the other one. Ripper was sorting things. Food, a medical kit, a few extra clips for his 9mm.

Du Pré got the .270 from the trunk. He lashed it, and the spotting scope, to the rear of the ORV.

Ripper looked at the nasty little machines.

"Fine-lookin' stock," he said. "What's this one's name? Whoa, boy."

The woman came out of the house with another blue five-gallon jug. She set it on the back of Ripper's machine and strapped it on with bungee cords.

"You going to the badlands?" she said.

Du Pré nodded.

"Drive over there to that ramp," she said. "I'll get the truck."

Du Pré and Ripper started their machines. Du Pré drove over to the loading ramp, a long tongue of earth with a sheer face of thick timbers. Mrs. Hulme came around the barn in a big old flatbed truck. It had no side skirts on the hood. The engine roared and spat. It had no muffler.

They drove the ORVs on to the flatbed and locked the brakes and the woman drove out of the main gate and turned left, went a mile and turned right. The road became a track and went through three dry watercourses and then over some sagebrush flats to a fence. There was a sagging gate in the fence.

And another loading ramp beside it.

Mrs. Hulme backed the truck up to the ramp and Ripper drove off and Du Pré followed him. The ramp was fairly steep and Ripper nearly went over backward at the bottom, from punching the gas too hard.

Mrs. Hulme stood by the open gate.

Du Pré stopped.

"Thank you," he said.

"It's those Host of Yahweh bastards," she said. It wasn't a question.

Du Pré nodded.

Du Pré drove on.

The badlands began.

They were colored, he thought, like rotting flesh and stinking bones.

CHAPTER 18

Du Pré sighted on Merritt Peak. He would use it to calculate where he was. He drove to the right of a small butte and roared on.

Cut her track five miles maybe.

But I do not know where she is going.

Can't go far fast, got them kids.

Got to get between her and them, they come after her sure.

The track was dust and then it was clay and then it was stones, round and polished by the wind. They could not go very fast. The land was broken and twisted by the wind and waters long gone.

They came to a rise that went to a knife ridge and at the top Du Pré stopped. He looked back at Merritt Peak, and then ahead at the strange jumbled rock.

Like a city ten thousand years old.

Some melted.

He looked off toward the Host of Yahweh ranch, but it was impossible to tell just where it lay.

Du Pré drove on, on dead reckoning.

Down in the bottoms it was impossible to tell where he was, and in a few moments he lost all sense of the landscape but what he could see left. Du Pré felt a prickling on the back of his neck.

It was a place of fears, a place unlike any other.

They came to a wide open cut in the land that led south and west. Du Pré stopped and he looked down.

Tracks of the wild horses.

Other tracks.

Cattle. A coyote.

Du Pré shut off his machine. He motioned to Ripper to do the same.

"God," said Ripper, "this is a miserable thing to drive. People do this for *fun?*"

Du Pré put his fingers in his ears to stop their popping. He swallowed and his right ear popped.

Neeeeeeeeeeeeeeeeeeeeeeee.

Du Pré cocked his ear.

The neeeeeeeeeeeeee sound was getting closer.

He started his machine and drove it down out of sight in a dry watercourse. Ripper followed.

They shut the machines off.

"She gets past," said Ripper, "you go after her. I will stay here and . . . discourage anyone who might wish to offer her assistance."

Du Pré snorted.

"So," said Ripper, "if you've no plans for that there rifle."

"It is not illegal," said Du Pré, "them drive in the badlands."

"Gabriel," said Ripper. "Two minutes after you find that woman it will be illegal for those bastards to be outside iron bars. I doubt she fled with her wee ones because she was forbidden to let them watch *Sesame Street*."

Du Pré took the rifle case from the back of his machine. He handed Ripper a box of twenty cartridges for it.

"Crosshairs they are dead on at two hundred yards."

Ripper nodded.

"That would mean an inch and a half low at three hundred and four at four hundred," he said.

Du Pré nodded.

Ripper opened the case and took out the rifle and filled the magazine and the chamber. He flicked the safety on and put the strap over his shoulder.

NEEEEEEEEEEEEEEEEEEEEEEEEE.

They looked through a cleft in the rocks.

The woman was driving fairly fast, and she had lost her bonnet and her long red hair whipped in the wind. She slowed and stared up at Merritt Peak for a moment, then she drove on. She passed within fifty feet of Du Pré and Ripper and then she was out of sight past a low cake of rock that stretched for a hundred yards to the northeast.

Du Pré nodded to Ripper.

Ripper touched his arm.

Engines, back to the south and west.

"Dirt bikes," said Ripper. "Some anyway. Faster than these things."

Du Pré nodded. He got on his machine and started it and drove up to the track the woman had gone down, turned and put the throttle all the way up.

In three minutes he could see her up ahead. She was driving as fast as she could. The children strapped on the back of the little machine were screaming and crying.

God damn, I wish she would blow a tire.

Engine seize up.

Du Pré followed, not knowing what to do.

The wide way narrowed down and the ground got rocky and the ORV bounced over the stones. Du Pré was only fifty yards behind the woman now.

She never looked back. She did not dare take her eyes off the ground right in front of her.

Du Pré kept the same distance.

They drove on deeper into the badlands.

She slowed down and stopped. She had come to a deep cut in the earth. She looked to the left and the right and then turned and drove right and she went down and then up and was moving fast again.

Du Pré went to the same spot and he dipped down and came up and opened the throttle.

She slowed again and this time she moved her head round far enough to spot Du Pré.

She turned immediately and gunned the engine, shot off a bank and disappeared from sight. Then she reappeared, a cloud of white dust marking the spot where she had landed.

Du Pré went the same way. He flew off the bank and landed on the dusty floor of the watercourse and he gunned the machine and shot up the grade.

She was fifty yards ahead again.

She looked back and speeded up.

Du Pré dropped back.

She was going too fast for the land.

She looked back again and slowed a little.

Du Pré waved.

She waited while Du Pré drove up to her.

The woman got off the ORV. She went to her babies and pulled the bungees from them and picked them up, one in each arm. They were perhaps four and two. Boys.

"We will help you," said Du Pré.

The woman looked at him with her wide brown eyes.

She put her children down.

She made a motion with her hand, like she was using a syringe.

She pointed to her mouth.

She stuck the imaginary needle in her tongue.

"You can't talk?" said Du Pré. "They give you a shot, your tongue?"

She nodded.

She knelt to comfort her children, who were crying. They were scared and hurt.

Du Pré looked on.

Numb her tongue up why?

So she can't talk.

The children blubbered.

She wiped their faces with a kerchief.

Du Pré heard a motorcycle engine. It was near.

A man on a dirt bike came out of a side cut, seeming to appear from the land.

The woman looked at him.

He was dressed in the baggy dark red shirt of the Host. He had on a black helmet with a dark visor.

The woman looked at Du Pré.

Her eyes looked tired and sad.

The man on the motorcycle gunned his engine and drove toward them.

The woman backed away, leaving her children crying, sitting on the ground.

Du Pré took out his 9mm. He raised his hand.

The man on the motorcycle stopped.

Du Pré turned to look at the woman.

She was still backing away.

She lifted her right hand.

She had a small pistol in it.

She put it to her temple and pulled the trigger.

CHAPTER 19

"I was her physician," said the man on the television, "and I was *held at bay* by an FBI agent! She was a deeply disturbed woman, and we wished only to keep her from inadvertently harming her children! The government seems to have *lost its mind.*"

"Doctor Vorbeck," said the pretty face, "it must have been terrible for you."

Harvey Wallace flicked off the sound.

"Way to go, team," he said. "Every paranoid asswipe in the country will be sleeping with their Kalashnikov tonight."

"It's a fucking crock, Harvey," said Ripper, "though I will have to admit it does look a bit unfavorable for us. Not the sort of thing I would choose to have on the airwaves."

"The director," said Harvey, "wants to set up an office in Antarctica. You will head it."

"That idiot?" said Ripper. "What's he got to do with this? I shook hands with the man once. Hardly a cause for misapprobation."

"His testicles," said Harvey, "are being deep-fat-fried by those morons who tried to impeach Clinton. His nuts hurt. He is somewhat obsessed with small matters, like the forty-'leven departmental regulations you pissed on. Like how bad it looks for the good old FBI to be engaged in kidnapping and waving guns at helpful citizens just trying to stop a crazy woman from doing herself and her children in. Like—"

"Want me to resign?" said Ripper.

"Noooooo," said Harvey, "matter of no interest to me whatever. The director's nuts are all hot and blistered. He could fire me, but then I'd sue his racist ass. You're another matter. You're one of *them*."

"He wouldn't—" said Ripper.

"He's gonna try to hang all this on you at the hearing," said Harvey.

"Well," said Ripper, "since I am clearly guilty of all the morons who tried to impeach Clinton accuse me of, I guess I can see his point."

"Smart boy," said Harvey. "Raised him from a pup."

"I will tell the naked and unappetizing truth," said Ripper.

"A good idea you're under oath," said Harvey.

"You two," said Madelaine, "quit makin' me laugh. I dropped a bead."

"It isn't funny," said Harvey.

"Fuck it isn't funny," said Madelaine. "You like it good enough."

"She sees through me," said Harvey. "The director and I cordially detest each other. Ask me, it's because we're so much alike."

Du Pré nodded. He sipped his whiskey.

"Could have been worse," he said.

Harvey looked at him.

"Could have shot the kids, too."

Tate's face was on the television. He was the father of the children, the husband of the woman who had shot herself. The woman who had told Du Pré she had been given a shot that paralyzed her tongue.

The autopsy had revealed traces of novocaine in her system. A Host of Yahweh dentist had sworn he had done some work on her that very morning.

"Yeah," said Harvey, "he could have. Ripper, you disappoint me."

"Sorry, Harvey," said Ripper.

"I believed in you," said Harvey. "Good old Ripper, I said to myself, he's treacherous, insubordinate, unscrupulous, clever, unprincipled, and reckless, but he's a genius, and he'll get me what I need."

"Think of the director's frying nuts, Harvey," said Ripper.

Harvey thought about it.

"Good boy," he said, "nice fella. Get you a milkbone. Now, what have you in mind to do, about these pukes here?"

"I'm thinking," said Ripper.

"I tell you you don't shut up I eighty-six you," said Madelaine.

Harvey looked at his ginger ale. Ripper looked abashed.

"Wanna dance, pretty lady?" said Harvey.

Madelaine nodded.

Du Pré laughed.

Madelaine stuck her needle in the purse she was beading and she came out from behind the bar and went to the jukebox, put in some quarters and punched some buttons.

Duke Ellington's orchestra made the music.

Harvey Weasel Fat and Madelaine Placquemines danced, elegantly.

"You don't dance?" said Ripper to Du Pré.

"I am always playing," said Du Pré. "I don't know how."

"Oh," said Ripper.

Harvey and Madelaine danced for twenty minutes, and then

Harvey bowed at the end of a song and Madelaine curtsied and Du Pré and Ripper applauded.

The pretty face on the television was saying something to a panel of gasbags who were to comment on the terrible events in Montana.

Madelaine switched the channel.

There were two teams playing baseball someplace.

She switched the channel again.

Professional wrestling.

One of the wrestlers broke a chair over the head of another. Then he grabbed another chair and flattened the referee. The crowd went wild.

"Ripper, Ripper," said Harvey, "whatcha gonna *do*? Save your old pal Harvey from early retirement. Pull the fat out of the fire. Now, Ripper, it would be a good idea you did something brilliant. Otherwise, I will make your life a misery. Your troubles will be my joys. I will bust your chops, you little *shit*!"

"Harvey," said Madelaine, "shut up. I am beading."

She looked at Ripper.

"You shut up, too," she said.

She looked at Du Pré.

"You can talk," she said.

Du Pré shrugged.

The door opened suddenly and a big man came in. He took off his dark glasses and waited a moment for his eyes to narrow in the dim light. It was a bright day.

Du Pré looked at him. He thought he knew him.

McPhie. The big highway patrolman from a couple hundred miles south of Toussaint. He wasn't in uniform.

McPhie came to the bar and nodded at Madelaine.

"Draft," said McPhie.

He looked at Du Pré.

"Gabriel," said McPhie, "how are ya keepin'?"

Du Pré nodded.

"Now," said McPhie, picking up his schooner, "could you tell me where I might find the head FBI prick?"

Du Pré looked at McPhie.

"That would be me," said Harvey.

"Good," said McPhie. "Now, a few days back Officer Parker stopped Du Pré there, and she was all concerned because Du Pré was actually not even over the speed limit, which is some forty miles per hour less'n he likes to drive at. It worried her, so she pulled out and went to see what might be wrong."

McPhie sucked down about half of his draft.

"When she approached the car," said McPhie, "she saw a subject in the back seat. She wasn't sure what the hell was going down. Then she saw the butt of an automatic, and so she pulled her weapon and ordered everyone to freeze."

McPhie sucked down the rest of his beer.

"Officers have to make split-second decisions," said McPhie, "and she did. It was to prove that the woman in the back seat was one Pidgeon, FBI agent."

Harvey's face was blank.

"Now," said McPhie, "one could look at this several ways, I suppose, but there isn't any evidence of intention on Parker's part to do wrong. Nevertheless, she has been suspended on a complaint from Agent Pidgeon, and she may well lose her job."

Harvey said nothing.

"Which is bullshit," said McPhie. "She's a good cop."

McPhie pushed his glass over the bar. He shook his head when Madelaine raised her eyebrows.

"I take it," said Harvey, "that you came to see the complaint withdrawn."

"Yes, indeedy," said McPhie.

Harvey nodded.

He stood up.

"Agent Pidgeon," said Harvey, "filed the complaint because

she felt Parker's judgment was poor. I trust Pidgeon's judgment."

McPhie nodded.

"You want help," he said, "you help."

CHAPTER

20

Du Pré parked his cruiser in the tall grass behind Benetsee's cabin. The rains had been good and the winter had lasted two weeks longer this year and the grama and bluebunch wheatgrass had shot up green and thick.

Du Pré looked at the big patch of sweetgrass near the sweat lodge. It was healthy and thick, too.

People plant the sweetgrass here, long time gone, Du Pré thought. Long time. They bring it from Asia.

Jesuits, they bring it from Europe. Peach cuttings, dandelions for the spring tonic, holy grass for the churches, scatter it on the floors.

Pelon was up on the roof fixing the leaks. He had on a red headband and old overalls. He stuck a broad scraper into thick black patching cement and daubed it places that let in water when it rained.

Du Pré rolled a smoke and walked up to the old cabin. The

roof came down low and there was a skirting so wood could be stacked out of the snow. Three panes of new glass sparked in the old window frames.

Benetsee maybe will be here now a while, Du Pré thought.

"I will be here," said Pelon. "Benetsee said he had to go to Canada."

"Why?" said Du Pré.

"Ceremonies," said Pelon, "or maybe he needed to get laid. Hell, I don't know. Somebody brought a bunch of stuff to fix the cabin with. He told me, Pelon, you are a good boy. I tell you a great secret, so you don't smash your thumb with the hammer. Hold the hammer, both hands, get Du Pré, hold the nail. Then he is gone. He goes down to the creek and into the willows and that is that."

Du Pré nodded. The old man came and went.

Go to Canada, turn into a bird and fly.

Du Pré laughed.

"Him, he run us pret' good," he said.

"No shit," said Pelon. "He said he is getting very tired and we have to do more work."

Their eyes met.

"Worries me," said Pelon. "He means he will die sometime."

Du Pré nodded.

"Old bastard," said Du Pré, "him, I got these questions for."

Pelon slapped a big gob of black cement on the roof.

"Him," said Pelon, "tell me you are too fat to think. Need to go and fast. Fat in your ears, fat in your nose, fat in your eyes. Things slip away from you."

Du Pré looked up at the butte where he had been several times, to fast and dream. The column of stone was high but not very wide. The dead heart of a long-vanished volcano, it was black basalt that broke into columns and fell in long pieces. The rubbled base looked like a huge stone woodpile.

"Him say anything else?" said Du Pré.

Pelon slapped on another gob of cement. He pushed it around with the scraper.

"Him say you need strong dreams," said Pelon. "He left something for you, the table next to the stove."

Du Pré nodded and he went into the cabin.

The blue feathers of a jay had been laid out in a circle on the table. The quills pointed to an old plastic pill bottle, white, the sort aspirin came in. Du Pré flipped up the top. There was a thick brown fluid in it, which smelled of bitter herbs.

Du Pré snorted. He put the lid back on the bottle.

"Think of the jay," said Pelon. He was hanging upside down from the roof and speaking through one of the new panes of glass.

"When he say I do this?" said Du Pré.

"Dark of the moon," said Pelon. "Tomorrow night maybe."

Du Pré nodded.

"I be here," he said. He put the little bottle in his pocket.

Pelon's head disappeared.

Du Pré walked outside.

"Him also said they don't find no gold but they are there," said Pelon. "That's all he say, I don't know what the hell he meant."

Du Pré nodded.

"Me, I don't know, either," said Du Pré.

"We find out," said Pelon, "and then he will show up. We maybe don't kill him by then."

Du Pré shook his head.

"Oh, yes," he said.

"We are ver' lucky," said Pelon.

Du Pré walked back to his cruiser, shaking his head.

He sat for a moment, having some whiskey and smoking. He stubbed the butt out on the side of his door and started the cruiser. When he glanced in the rearview mirror he could see Pelon glopping black patching cement on the roof.

Blue jay is a thief. Steals things, shiny things, steals from other birds, steals their eggs, steals the twigs they build their nests with.

Blue jay don't care, he just go *skraaak!*

Little crow.

Hop and look, cock his head.

Bright blue feathers.

Du Pré felt for the plastic bottle in his shirt pocket. It was there, and some of the tail feathers.

I don't put the tail feathers, my pocket.

Maybe I do.

Du Pré turned east and drove along the bench road clear to the east end of the Wolf Mountains, and then he picked up the road he and Ripper had come down the day they had tried to help the woman who ran from the Host of Yahweh compound.

He got to the gate at the Hulme ranch and turned in. There were two pickups and a dusty open jeep parked next to the house. Du Pré looked at his watch. Noon. The Hulmes would be eating.

Du Pré drove in and parked and got out. Mrs. Hulme came out the door.

"Du Pré!" she said, "can you eat? Carter and the boys are here now."

Carter and Marge Hulme, Du Pré thought. I am getting old I could not remember their names. Don't remember the kids'.

Du Pré followed her into the house and sat at the big kitchen table with Carter Hulme and his sons, both grown now, men in their early twenties.

"Lee and Billy," said Carter Hulme. Du Pré shook hands.

Marge Hulme put a beef sandwich in front of Du Pré and a tall glass of iced tea.

"Hell of a business t'other day," said Carter. " 'Bout all we need is a goddamned cult here, too."

The boys nodded.

"Fenced off the trail I use to move my cattle to summer pasture," said Hulme. "Been here all my life, next to the Eides, and now this. Takes me another five miles to get to my permits."

Du Pré nodded.

"Bud, Millie Eide are members," said Du Pré.

The table went dead silent.

"Goddamn," said Carter.

"Makes a few things make sense that don't," said Lee Hulme.

Marge sat down with her sandwich.

"Californians," she said.

Everyone nodded.

"They'll try to buy our place," said Billy quietly.

"Try," said Carter.

Du Pré laughed.

"I'd sell this place to the Devil and buy hell with the money," said Carter. "But not them. Never them."

Du Pré ate his sandwich. Good beef and mustard.

"Who knows them badlands good," said Du Pré.

"Billy," said Carter. "Ever since he was a shaver, he's been goin' out there."

Du Pré nodded.

"He spent three weeks out there once," said Marge. "Left the day before school started. We thought he was *dead.*"

"I was fine, Ma," said Billy. "I just hated school."

"I am looking for something," said Du Pré.

Billy looked at him.

"Spanish mine," said Du Pré.

Billy shook his head, but he hesitated before he did.

CHAPTER
21

"I see," said Foote. "Very interesting."

"They got satellites, take photographs," said Du Pré.

"Arrastras," said Foote.

"Like big stone wheels," said Du Pré, "maybe they don't use them, but maybe they do. If there were some, there would be circles in the earth, maybe twenty feet across. Mule, horse, they pull the shaft the wheel crushes the ore."

"What are the coordinates again?" said Foote.

Du Pré read him the numbers from the topographical maps. The maps weren't very accurate.

"I'll see what I can find," said Foote. "And may I speak to Bart for a moment?"

Du Pré handed the cell phone to Bart. He walked away from the conversation.

They were standing outside the Toussaint Saloon. There were dark lines on the western horizon.

I got to go the butte tonight and it will rain on me.

Thank you, Benetsee.

I put ipecac, your wine, next time.

Bart finished and he shut up the cell phone and put it in his shirt pocket.

"I be gone maybe two three days," said Du Pré. "He said he would see, call back."

Bart nodded.

"Hard news about the Eides," said Bart. "Things get tough, people go crazy. I did." He laughed.

Du Pré grinned.

"Well," said Bart, "I am off to tear a new irrigation ditch for the Martins. Morgan Martin is diversifying. She's gonna have a huge patch of *mint*."

Lots of ranchers did that, the oil was valuable, used in some odd industrial processes. The mint had to be cropped and processed almost continually, so an acre was a lot.

Du Pré looked at Bart.

"Hundred and ten acres," said Bart. "Wear out a lot of blades mowin' it, she will." He laughed and went off to his eighteen-wheeler, which had twenty-six, because Popsicle, his lime-green dragline, weighed nearly fifty tons.

Du Pré went into the saloon. Madelaine was beading.

"Get your own drink, Du Pré," she said, staring at the little purse. "Get a big one, you don't have any next two, three days."

Du Pré went behind the bar and he made a tall stiff ditch. He went back round and sat across from Madelaine. She pulled the thread tight and she set down the purse.

"Benetsee is good for you," she said. "It take maybe five years for you, figure that out, but he is good for you."

Du Pré snorted.

"You ask that Foote, the satellite maps?" she said. She lit a cigarette. Someone had left a pack of long brown filter tips on the bar.

"Yah," said Du Pré, "that Hulme kid, he knows where this is. Don't want anyone else to know."

"His place," said Madelaine.

Du Pré nodded.

"Go and talk to him, Du Pré," said Madelaine. "You find it on your own, maybe he go crazy, put a bullet in you."

Du Pré noded.

"Yah," he said. He got up.

"They fire that Parker cop," said Madelaine. "I didn't think it was bad enough, do that."

Du Pré shrugged.

"Be back, dinner," said Madelaine. "Last dinner you get, a while."

Du Pré leaned far over the bar and they kissed. He went out the door with his ditch in his hand.

It took forty minutes to get to the Hulmes. There was only one pickup by the house. Du Pré got out and looked around.

Somebody was grinding something in the machine shed.

Du Pré walked over and looked in. A stream of sparks fell from a whirling carborundum disc. Billy Hulme was working on a big part. The air stank of welded metal. Du Pré waited until Billy put down the grinder and flipped up his mask.

"Billy," said Du Pré.

Billy did not start and he did not look at Du Pré.

"I need your help," said Du Pré.

Billy looked at him then.

"I don't want nothing from there," said Du Pré.

"You were already there, you son of a bitch," said Billy.

Du Pré shook his head.

"Not me," he said.

Billy pulled off his heavy leather gloves and slammed them down on the workbench.

"No," said Du Pré.

"Somebody was," said Billy. "They came on a dirt bike."

123

"Eides maybe," said Du Pré. "Bud and Millie, I saw them, they are part of that Host of Yahweh."

"No shit," said Billy.

"You take me there," said Du Pré. "I find it anyway someday, but it is yours, you found it first."

Billy looked at Du Pré.

"OK," he said. "It's hard. It was mine and no one else knew about it."

Your mother know about it, thought Du Pré. Them women they know everything.

"Come on," said Billy. He walked out of the machine shed, tossing his long leather welder's apron on a barrel.

He got in the pickup. Du Pré got in, too, and Billy started the truck and drove down toward the back pasture to the gate where the badlands began.

Billy picked his way expertly through the maze, through places Du Pré wasn't sure that the truck would fit. He worked the truck south and east. A couple of times Du Pré could see the lands of the host ranch in the distance.

"This was their old cart trail," said Billy. "They made charcoal up in the mountains and brought it down here to roast the ore."

Long time gone, Du Pré thought. Early 1600s?

Billy parked the truck and they got out. They were in a hidden hole, a place where the earth seemed to have sunk in a circle as though it had been cut by a knife. The walls around the circle were only ten to fifteen feet high.

Water belled nearby.

"Spring over there," said Billy, "so they had water. The water runs about forty feet and goes back into the earth. Mine's over there."

Du Pré looked at the far side of the hole. There was some scrubby sagebrush and a single juniper writhing up out of rock.

Billy began to walk.

Du Pré smiled.

A door. Weathered the same pale gray as the rock it was set against.

So dry here the door had lasted for centuries.

Billy went to it and lifted it and set it aside. It was so dessicated that it was light as Styrofoam.

The mine shaft was only the size of a door on a house. Billy turned on a flashlight and he went in.

There was a room twenty feet back, perhaps thirty feet across.

Billy put the light on some rusty metal.

Du Pré squinted.

Rusty armor.

"Four of 'em," said Billy. "Most of the bones are gone. Coyotes took 'em maybe. That bastard was here at least didn't take anything."

Billy put the light on a flat slab of rock. Four swords lay there, the leather fittings on the scabbards dried to dark twists.

"That's the vein," said Billy. "The raster wheels are outside, but they were cracked, so frost busted them up."

Du Pré nodded.

He took a spool of yellow plastic tape from his pocket.

"I put this over the entrance," said Du Pré.

Du Pré pulled off a few feet of the tape.

DO NOT ENTER POLICE INVESTIGATION said the tape, over and over.

"I liked it better when it was just me," said Billy.

"Yah," said Du Pré.

CHAPTER
22

It began to rain as Du Pré walked up the path to the top of the butte back of Benetsee's cabin. He could drive to the base of the formation on an old logging road and then scramble up the steep path. The rocks and soil got slick and his bootsoles slipped and he cursed and grabbed for handholds.

The rain fell in sheets and Du Pré was soaked through. Runnels of water ran down his back and his ass and slid down his legs. His feet squelched in his boots.

"Good cold wind now I die up here, you old prick," said Du Pré to the water, air, and earth.

He sat on a rock and watched the silver rain fall from all the low points on his clothes. Rain ran off the end of his nose. It itched.

He felt in his shirt pocket for the little pill bottle. He took it out and smelled the bitter contents.

Fuck, he thought, and he drank it.

It smelled bitter but tasted sweet, like balsam.

He tried to roll a cigarette but the rain was too much and the papers shredded in his fingers.

"Man here in this, pret' stupid man," said Benetsee. He had come and he sat not six inches from Du Pré on the rock. He was soaked, too, but he grinned happily.

Du Pré glared at him.

"Come," said Benetsee. He walked to the edge of the butte and stepped down a path that Du Pré had never seen before. It was easy to walk on even in the rain, and soon they were on level ground and near Du Pré's cruiser.

They got in.

Du Pré burped. The sweetish taste was pleasant, woody and thick.

"Old man," said Du Pré, "one day I just shoot you. I do that."

Benetsee laughed for a long time.

"You be lost then," he said.

Du Pré nodded grimly, started the car and drove off to Benetsee's cabin. He had to go out to the county road on one track and back to the cabin on another. The rain sluiced down very hard and Du Pré could barely see out the windshield even with the wipers set at their fastest.

He stopped the car and shut it off and then ran toward the cabin. There was a warm yellow light inside. The stove was hot and the air warm and dry.

Pelon was sitting at the little table.

Water was running in a small stream down from the board ceiling into a bucket on the floor.

"No good," said Benetsee. "You miss something."

Pelon nodded glumly.

"Our good friend brings us wine, tobacco, meat," said Benetsee.

Du Pré clenched his teeth. It was all in the trunk of the car, out in the driving rain. His clothes had already begun to steam.

He went back out and stomped angrily to the cruiser. He

got the trunk open and fished out the plastic bags with the wine and food and tobacco in them. He got his whiskey from under the front seat, and a change of dry clothes in another plastic bag.

He squelched back to the house in his sodden clothes and boots. Benetsee was sitting on the chair that Pelon had been on. He looked perfectly dry and comfortable.

Du Pré set down the bags. He reached for the big jug of screwtop wine, opened it, and poured Benetsee a quart jar full. The old man grinned and took the jar and drank it all in one long swallow.

Du Pré looked around the tiny cabin.

"Where is Pelon?" he said.

"Up on the roof fixing the leak," said Benetsee.

"In this shit?" said Du Pré.

"He do it first time up there he not be there now," said Benetsee.

Du Pré looked at the silver thread of water running from the ceiling to the bucket.

"Pret' hard to tell where that is, this," he said.

"Pelon got to learn," said Benetsee, "see things that are hard to see."

Du Pré had some whiskey. He stripped off his soggy clothes and hung them on a cord that stretched across the room near the stove. He stood naked with his back to the heat until he was dry. The fire in the stove crackled and popped and the air whistled through the little cracks where the pieces of cast iron joined.

Du Pré put on his dry clothes. He put his boots on some long pegs near the chimney. They began to steam.

He sat at the table and got a package of tobacco and rolled a smoke for each of them. His shepherd's lighter was so wet it would not work. He took a match from a saucer on the table and struck it and lit his smoke, then held the flame out to Benetsee. The old man bent his head to the light.

They smoked.

"Good tobacco," said Benetsee.

Du Pré looked at the package. Holland.

"Dutch," said Du Pré.

"Good people," said Benetsee.

"I am supposed, have a vision," said Du Pré. "I go like you say, the butte."

"Pret' lousy weather," said Benetsee. "Me, I would have it here."

The silver thread of water slowed and stopped.

Pelon had found the leak.

"Him," said Benetsee, "got to learn things."

"Him, manage to stay alive around you," said Du Pré, "he learn plenty."

Benetsee laughed and laughed.

"Dumb shits," he said, "both, you."

"What is that stuff I drank?" said Du Pré.

"Peru balsam," said Benetsee.

Balsam of Peru, Du Pré thought. My people are a long way from Peru.

"Spanish mine," said Benetsee.

Du Pré nodded.

"I go there this afternoon," said Du Pré.

"What you need a vision for then?" said Benetsee.

Du Pré rubbed his eyes.

This old man is always telling me something, won't tell me anything.

Pelon came in, water streaming from his clothes. He looked at the place in the ceiling where the leak had been.

"There," said Pelon.

"Get dry," said Benetsee.

Pelon stripped and put his wet clothes on nails and the cord and he fished some dry clothes out of a box under the bed. He was shivering. He went to the stove and stood next to it.

Du Pré started to offer him the whiskey but remembered

that Pelon didn't drink alcohol. Pelon made himself some tea. He stood close to the stove sipping the hot liquid.

Benetsee drank more wine.

Du Pré rolled them two more smokes. He lit both and he handed one to Benetsee.

"What am I not seeing, old man," said Du Pré.

Benetsee grinned.

His brown stumps of teeth showed just above his lower lip.

"What is the blue jay?" said Du Pré.

Benetsee grinned.

"What I do about this Host of Yahweh?" said Du Pré.

"Bad people," said Benetsee. "Lots of guns, explosives."

Du Pré looked at him.

"Who is the White Priest?" said Du Pré.

Benetsee looked away for a long time. Then he nodded.

"Why they give that woman a shot, her tongue don't work?"

"Shit," said Pelon. He was looking at the ceiling.

Water was dripping from the place it had leaked from before.

Benetsee laughed.

Pelon shrugged.

"I don't go up there again," he said.

"You smart," said Benetsee, "you don't go up there the first time."

Pelon nodded.

"I am angry," he said. "I go up there because I am angry."

He sipped tea.

"Help me, old man," said Du Pré.

"Spanish mine," said Benetsee.

Du Pré looked at him.

"I been there," said Du Pré.

Benetsee put out his smoke.

"No, you haven't," he said. "You go the wrong one."

"Shit," said Du Pré, "there are two, them?"

Benetsee nodded.

CHAPTER
23

"Him don't know," said Du Pré.

Old man, he knows the riddles but sometimes he doesn't know the answers.

At least he knows the riddles.

"Benetsee sees farther," said Madelaine, "things they are not so clear then."

Du Pré coughed. His mouth still tasted of balsam of Peru.

Catfoot once had a bad cut got infected, he put that balsam of Peru on it, all the proud flesh went away. Like using sugar on a wire cut on a horse or a cow.

Them Spanish miners, they carry it, pack bad wounds with.

Long time gone.

Madelaine ran her fingernail over Du Pré's chest.

"You pret' good in bed, an old fart," she said.

Du Pré snorted.

The window in the bedroom was open and the thick scent

of lilacs poured in. There had been a hard frost when they first bloomed, and so they grew and bloomed again.

"Wonder why they do that, that woman's tongue," said Madelaine.

"They are mean bastards," said Du Pré.

"They are *smart* mean bastards," said Madelaine, "can't speak can't yell pret' well ties you up."

Du Pré nodded. He yawned and got up and went to take a piss.

When he got back, Madelaine was sitting on the edge of the bed in her flowered robe, combing her long black hair. She had silver streaks in it. Bright silver.

"Ripper he is back today," said Madelaine.

"Where he go?" said Du Pré.

"California," said Madelaine. "He tell me let you know but nobody else."

"So you let me know he is back?" said Du Pré.

"You got other things, your mind," said Madelaine. "Me, I think you maybe notice he is gone. It is quiet, then, maybe you say, hey, why is it not noisy? Oh, that Ripper is gone, is why."

Du Pré laughed.

"They got guns," said Du Pré. "They got them hid someplace."

"So?" said Madelaine.

"Automatic weapons," said Du Pré, "military stuff."

"So do you," said Madelaine, "so do lots of people. Old Henry Wyrie him got a *cannon*."

Du Pré nodded.

Yeah, old Henry him have a 20mm cannon, rapid-fire. Everybody know that, but no one want to drive up, his house, say, "Old Henry, you are a bad guy, bring out your cannon, we arrest you." Old Henry, him don't like nosy people.

"That Waco," said Madelaine. "There are children, mothers there. It is so dumb, they send in that tank. All they got to do, is wait. Like them dumb Freemen, just wait."

"Yah," said Du Pré.

"Ripper," said Madelaine, "him don't like to wait."

"Ripper," said Du Pré, "he is pretty crazy. Not stupid. Them FBI, Waco, they are stupid, is all."

"Them children, mothers, people, are dead, is all," said Madelaine.

"I make us coffee," said Du Pré.

"I tell you, Du Pré," said Madelaine, "you don't get mad this time. You have plenty reason, get mad. But you don't do it."

"OK," said Du Pré.

"Bullshit, OK," said Madelaine. "You think about that Waco and you don't be stupid. You are pretty smart, for a man."

Du Pré laughed. He put on his clothes and boots and walked to the kitchen. He put on water to heat and filled the French press with coffee. He set put two cups and filled the creamer with milk. He put a spoon next to Madelaine's cup. She liked milk and sugar in her coffee.

The shower went on. It wasn't on very long. Madelaine had raised four kids in this little house, with one bathroom. She was very clean and very fast at it.

Girl in college in California and all three boys in the military.

They don't come back much, like my Maria.

Du Pré grinned, thinking of his daughter.

He drank coffee.

"That Maria she is coming, you know," said Madelaine. "She call, I forget to tell you."

"Maria," said Du Pré.

How the hell she know I am thinking of my daughter.

"You get that one smile you are thinking of her," said Madelaine. "You got another, Jacqueline. One for me, too."

"That is good," said Du Pré.

"Yah," said Madelaine, rubbing her hair with a thick cream towel, "it is ver' good, that."

Du Pré laughed.

"That Parker cop, she is fired, pulling a gun," said Madelaine. "It is fake. She work that out, Pidgeon."

Du Pré was drinking coffee. He was startled, and some ran down his chin and dripped on the front of his shirt.

"Sorry," said Madelaine, "I forget you shock so easy."

"What, this?" said Du Pré.

"Them Host of Yahweh," said Madelaine, "they can get a cop, join, she is fired, they like that, think they got something."

"They are pretty smart," said Du Pré.

"Yeah," said Madelaine, "they know it, too, makes them foolish. Thing I like about you, Du Pré, is even when you are being smart you don't piss yourself you are so pleased."

Du Pré laughed.

"How you figure this all out?"

"Parker, she is five foot, blond, pretty," said Madelaine. "She got to be one tough smart lady, get to be a Highway patrol officer. No way she is stupid enough, pull a gun got no reason."

"I am driving too slow," said Du Pré.

"Cause the Pidgeon she is bitching," said Madelaine, "she and that Parker, they talk."

Du Pré mopped the wet spots on his shirt.

"Go and get another shirt," said Madelaine. "That one, people will think I don't take good care of you."

"Coffee stains?" said Du Pré.

"My reputation we are talking, Du Pré," said Madelaine, "so go."

Du Pré went to the closet and got out a clean shirt. He put the stained one in the laundry hamper and put the clean shirt on.

Coffee stains.

Du Pré went back down to the kitchen. Madelaine was bent over the sink, rubbing her hair with the herbs she gathered and dried and put in little muslin bags.

Clover, wild thyme, and some Du Pré didn't know.

"So," said Madelaine, rubbing, "now you keep your mouth

shut, she is going to do ver' dangerous thing. Don't tell that damn Ripper. He will charge in there, waving a sword or something."

Du Pré laughed.

Ripper had gone to arrest some dopers dressed as the Mad Hatter.

Harvey said he had gone into a warehouse after a shooter once in a costume that made him look like the mean creature in *Alien*. The shooter was so stunned he dropped his gun.

Ripper was crazy.

Brave, too.

"Tongue thing it bothers me," said Madelaine. "They maybe do that to all them women."

"I heard one speak," said Du Pré.

Madelaine nodded.

"One," she said. "One is not a lot."

Du Pré looked away. He saw the woman who had run into the badlands, backing away from Tate, putting the little pistol to her temple.

Pop, the gun said.

The woman stood still for a moment.

Then she began to tremble all over.

She fell and gasped for a long time.

She died.

Tate's kids had screamed.

They would remember it even if they were too young to know what it meant.

"You snap your shirt wrong," said Madelaine.

Du Pré looked down, to see he had.

He pulled the row of snaps apart.

He snapped his snaps in proper order.

"That's better," said Madelaine.

CHAPTER

24

"Everybody got their popcorn and jujubes?" said Ripper. "Big leaky paper cups of watery pop?" He had picked up a Host of Yahweh recruiting tape on his California trip.

"Put the fucking tape in," said Harvey. "One more word outta you and you go to your room without any fresh blood for supper."

Ripper grinned. He stuck the tape in the VCR. A massed chorus sang Handel. The picture was a rapid montage of beautiful sunsets, sunrises, and lots of fat white clouds scooting across a blue sky.

"To be the best that we can be," said a fat voice, "to the glory of God and to the eternal wisdoms, the Prophets here, now, and among us . . ."

Flights of flamingoes took off from a marsh. A bald eagle twisted its white head and the camera zoomed in on its yellow eye.

"We wish only to be the best that we can be," said the fat voice.

A smiling young couple dressed in mountain-climbing gear looked up a sheer rock face. They looked at each other with dripping affection, then started to climb it in the wrong place.

"The clouds, the poultry, the precipice," said Ripper, in his deepest voice.

"Shaddup," said Harvey.

"The Host of Yahweh is the fruit of God's healing," said the fat voice, "for all of us were once in terrible pain, addicted, isolated, miserable, lost, far from God."

The young couple in the climbing gear were on the rock face about fifteen feet from the ground, grinning joyously.

"Don't know fuck-all about it," said Ripper. "Ah, Hollywood."

"SHUT THE FUCK UP!" roared Harvey.

Ripper grinned evilly at his boss.

The film changed to a massed chorus of men, women, and children holding hymnals, hands, and massed joyous smiles. The men all wore the old-blood-colored baggy shirts and black pants, the women long gray dresses and bonnets, and the children miniatures of their parents' costumes.

The picture changed to a city street, where well-dressed people were marching toward some appointment or other. They were passing some ragged beggars, pitiably holding out their hands palms up. Some passersby put coins in the hands.

The beggars were dirty, but the dirt had been painted on. They got up and sneaked off. They bought drugs from a leering dealer. The dealer took one of the women beggars into a room while the others smoked and snorted.

A shot of hands sticking out of the bars of cells.

A shot of prison walls.

The beggars were back at their station, looking beseeching. A beautiful young woman in a long gray dress and bonnet came to them and she smiled winningly.

A light shone down upon her.

The beggars followed her.

They appeared in the middle of the bellowing chorus of costumed people, who smiled benevolently at them and shared their hymnals.

The beggars bellowed, too.

The beautiful young couple grinned down from thirty feet up the rock face.

They had been the beggars. The woman had been taken to the back room by the leering dope dealer.

The dope dealer was singing with the throng, and he was cleaned up and wearing the odd shirt.

"We only wish to be the best that we can," said the fat voice.

Picture of a schoolroom rich in computers, each with a pair of scrubbed, smiling children in front of the screen.

The teacher was the woman who had been taken by the dope dealer before embarking on the rock face. She smiled radiantly at the children, who smiled back happily.

"Our home schools are the best in America," said the fat voice.

Picture of Host of Yahweh people picking oranges and handing the fruit down carefully, all the while smiling radiantly.

A Host of Yahweh man sat on a huge tractor, plowing up black earth.

Picture of a burning dump somewhere. Old cars, appliances, bags of trash.

Shot of an oil slick on water.

Shot of a bird covered in oil.

Shot of a huge redwood tree falling.

Shot of power-plant smokestacks belching white streamers.

Shot of a superhighway filled with cars, all crawling at half a mile an hour.

Shot of a small white seal being whacked over the head.

"Our planet, Mother Earth, is ill," said the fat voice.

Back to the chorus.

Shot of the woman with the fixed smile feeding a baby raccoon.

"The goddamned raccoons where I live steal my *mail*," said Harvey. "They are about as endangered as goddamned dandelions."

Shot of happy Host of Yahweh people cleaning debris out of a creek.

Shot of leaping salmon.

"The Host of Yahweh," said the fat voice, "will heal Mother Earth's wounds . . ."

The chorus bellowed.

The woman with the fixed smile waved down from the rock face.

She stuck the nipple of a milk bottle into the mouth of a baby goat.

She grinned wide.

The chorus bellowed.

"We are not alone in this Universe," said the fat voice.

Shot of the gigantic stone figures built by Indians on the dry Chilean plains.

"The Wise walk among us," said the fat voice.

Shot of a man in white robes, standing on a rock by the sea. He held his arms out and turned the palms of his hands face up.

"But one must listen . . ." said the fat voice.

The man in the white robes stood with his head humbly bowed.

Weird electronic music throbbed.

Shot of a starry sky.

"There are so many worlds," said the fat voice.

"There is the Force of Good," said the fat voice.

The chorus, the smiling woman feeding the raccoon, the people cleaning out the creek.

"And the Force of Darkness," said the fat voice.

142

Belching smokestacks.

An oil slick on the ocean waves.

The man in the white robes turned to the camera, and the sea swelled behind him.

His face was entirely swaddled. There was just a slit in the headdress for his eyes.

"The Wise walk among us," said the fat voice.

The man in the white robes looked heavenward.

"There is our salvation," said a distorted and mechanical voice. "In the heavens they are watching . . ."

The man in the white robes watched the heavens.

"I have been honored," said the weird voice, "with three visitations."

The starry sky, black and twinkling with lights. A red light moved across the heavens.

It went right to left and then left to right.

"Three times," said the mechanical voice.

The man in the white robes stood on his rock by the roaring ocean.

Shot of waves crashing into rocks.

"My heart was hard, though," said the mechanical voice.

The man in the white robes stood defiantly.

"But they loved me," said the mechanical voice.

Shot of the starry heavens.

"They came for me," said the mechanical voice.

Shot of the pounding sea.

Shot of the starry heavens.

"In their spaceship," said the man in the white robes.

"They loved me and did not rebuke me . . ."

"I flew high above the world . . ."

"I received their wisdom . . ."

"It is yours for the asking . . ."

Swelling chorus.

"Bless you all," said the mechanical voice, "from the Wise . . ."

Swelling chorus of Host of Yahweh singers.

"And their humble servant . . ."

The man in white stood by the sea.

The film ended.

"My, my," said Ripper. "My, my, my."

CHAPTER

25

Du Pré peered and rubbed his eyes.

Maps of the badlands lay on the big table in Bart's house. The maps were probably wrong. The Forest Service maps of the Wolf Mountains were known locally as "the funny papers."

Squiggles. Elevations.

The land was a wind-carved jumble. A surveying crew would have revolted. Like the one that was surveying the border between Montana and Idaho, along the crests of the ridges in the mountains. It began to rain. The surveying crew got drunk, pointed their instruments due north, and did not stop until they came to the Canadian border.

That part of the boundary was still a straight line, silly in a land of folded, faulted mountains and big rivers that were older than the mountains were.

Rivers are almost always older than the mountains they flow through, Du Pré thought. I could not believe it when I was told that. Later I believed it. Them scientists are wrong a lot but Benetsee never is.

"Rock is hard," said Benetsee once, "water soft, time is very long. Rock never win."

They had been standing in the bed of the old Missouri River, which a long time gone had flowed to Hudson's Bay, after joining the Red River of the North.

Benetsee pointed to the old shoreline. It had snowed the night before, and the old shores stood out like dusted fingerprints do.

Long time gone.

Where the fuck's the other mine? Du Pré thought.

He stared at the maps.

He rubbed his eyes.

Bullshit this is.

The telephone rang.

Du Pré looked at the machine.

He got up and went to it and he hesitated.

Might be for Bart.

Du Pré lifted up the phone.

"I am trying to reach Mr. Gabriel Du Pré," said a voice, young and tense.

"It is me," said Du Pré.

"I believe I have some information for you. I am not going to identify myself. You were interested in features in the landscape at roughly the southeast corner of the Wolf Mountains of Montana. I was told you wished any evidences of old mining activity. Specifically, circular tracks . . ."

"Yah," said Du Pré.

"There are two sets," said the voice. "One at . . ."

The voice recited latitude and longitude. Du Pré scribbled down numbers.

"Got those coordinates?" said the voice.

"Yes," said Du Pré.

The line went dead.

Du Pré put the phone back in its cradle and he went to the maps spread out on the table. He set them together and found the place in the badlands he had gone to with Billy Hulme.

The other numbers weren't on the maps.

The degrees were the same but the minutes and seconds were less for both latitude and longitude.

"Son of a bitch!" said Du Pré.

He rolled up the maps and tucked them in a big mailing tube and put them in the closet in his room. He went out to his old cruiser and drove to Toussaint.

Madelaine was tending the bar tonight. Susan Klein had had to go to Billings to get a wisdom tooth pulled. The dentist she went to nearby wouldn't touch it.

There were ten or so people in the bar, drinking ditches and beers and chaffing each other.

Nobody looked twice at Du Pré when he came in.

Madelaine pulled a couple of beers. She set them in front of the customers and she had change from the cash on the bartop. Then she came down the bar to Du Pré.

Madelaine studied his face.

"OK," she said, "Du Pré is worried."

He glanced back at the room. No one was looking at them.

"That mine," he said, "it is on the Eide place. There were two of them."

Madelaine nodded.

She looked at him again.

"Them Eide," she said, "they join that bunch. When?"

Du Pré nodded.

"Ripper," said Du Pré, "he is in the back?"

Madelaine nodded.

"Left here, twenty minutes ago," she said.

"I be back," said Du Pré.

He went out the back door of the saloon and stopped for a

moment and looked up at the sky. A meteor streaked brilliant green across the deep blue and the line of strange light went down over the horizon.

He knocked on the door of the room Ripper had rented.

Ripper opened it before Du Pré's knuckles struck a second time.

Du Pré stepped inside.

Ripper said nothing. He looked carefully at Du Pré's face.

"There are two old Spanish mines," said Du Pré. "One, that Hulme kid found. Other one, it is on the Eide ranch someplace. That is the one the guns are in."

Ripper sighed.

"They were moved here before the sale," he said, "before the Eides left. Very nice."

"Benetsee, he see them," said Du Pré. "He just don't know which mine, don't know, there are two of them, which one has the guns."

Ripper nodded.

He laughed.

"There is magic in the world," he said. "We have got that at least."

"Eides, they don't sell to Bart, now we know why," said Du Pré.

Ripper waved to a chair. He pointed to a bottle of Scotch.

Du Pré shook his head.

"Harvey will be back about noon tomorrow," said Ripper. "He's been after all the Eides who didn't join the Host. Bud and Millie owned the place. The others were family, but only that."

Du Pré nodded.

Two other smaller places near the Wolf Mountains had been owned by Eides, but they were too small to live on, so they had sold out and gone to the main ranch owned by more prosperous members of the family.

Du Pré sighed.

"Happens," said Ripper. "People, they lose things they love, the world changes and makes no sense, so they find explanations. Too bad the Eides found this one. But they did. You know more'n three million Americans think they were abducted by aliens? That scares me more'n dope and Ross Perot."

Du Pré laughed.

"You like that videotape?" said Ripper. "The masked man on the rock? The Guy Who Knows. Terrifying."

"You don't got nothing, them guns?" said Du Pré.

Ripper shook his head.

"Nothing direct," he said, "though there was one theft, a break-in at a National Guard armory, that we've never been able to solve. The thieves got away with two hundred assault rifles, some antitank stuff—those plastic bazookas, use 'em and toss, grenades, light machine guns, and some plastic explosives. Good haul. Usually somebody rats out on something like that, when they get busted for something and they want the judge to have an attack of the kindlies. But other'n the usual lies everybody tells when they land in the can, nothing."

"Where?" said Du Pré.

"Los Angeles," said Ripper. "We were worried enough so we took tea with the local bad guys. They apologized. As loyal Americans, they feared terrorists, which they do, being your basic Republican businessmen. They had made inquiries, and got nothing."

Du Pré nodded.

"That Host did it," he said.

"Sure," said Ripper. "Did a good job, too. Nothing to go to a judge with and say, my man, I would like a search warrant."

"I find it," said Du Pré.

"I didn't hear that," said Ripper. "Like I'm not asking you if you might know anything about demolitions."

Du Pré shook his head.

Yes.

CHAPTER
26

Du Pré stared down from the window of the little plane. He fixed his eyes on a barely perceptible broad line on the land below.

He looked at his map.

He stared at the line.

Then he looked out of the other window. The badlands lay there, their washed-out dead colors even paler in the haze. By afternoon the winds had lifted tons of dust into the air.

"OK," said Du Pré.

"You see what you need to?" said Bart.

Du Pré nodded.

The pilot flew back to the small airstrip in the field across the road from the Toussaint saloon. He set the fat-tired plane down. When he came to a stop, Du Pré and Bart got out and the pilot nodded to them. As soon as they were fifty feet away, he gunned the engine and turned the plane around and went down the dirt runway and was airborne in seconds.

"The gold and silver is in that reef," said Du Pré, "comes up in the badlands, almost comes up on the Eide ranch. Them Spanish, they are pret' good miners, find that out on the prairie."

"Didn't do them a lot of good," said Bart.

Du Pré nodded. No way of knowing which Indians had been here then, in the early 1600s, late 1500s, but they had killed the Spanish miners. The Spanish had good armor but not good enough.

"Amazing that they made it this far north," said Bart.

Du Pré nodded.

They walk a long way for that gold. There is much more gold over in Alder Gulch but they never find that.

"I couldn't see anything," said Bart.

Du Pré rolled a smoke.

"It is there," he said. "You see that reef, a line in the grass, the land a little higher there?"

Bart looked at Du Pré.

"I'd go with you," he said.

Du Pré shook his head.

"I go alone," said Du Pré. "I got to be quiet."

Bart nodded.

"If you change your mind," he said.

Du Pré nodded. He smoked. He looked away.

Bart went off to his truck, whistling.

Du Pré laughed.

Bart was very brave, but very noisy. Once he had gone hunting with Du Pré, and he made so much noise all the game left for the other side of the Wolf Mountains.

Bart, him don't like to hunt. Good thing, too.

Harvey Wallace sauntered around the corner of the saloon, his big hands thrust deep in his pockets. He was shaking his head very slowly, thinking careful thoughts.

When he got close to Du Pré, he looked up and he nodded.

"Afternoon," he said. He looked off toward the Wolf Mountains.

"What?" said Du Pré.

Harvey looked at him.

"I talked to several of the Eides," said Harvey. "Seems that when beef fell and the weather got good and dry, which it does in Montana more often than not, Bud and Millie got very religious. They went to that Bible Fellowship church over in Cooper. Watched Christian television. Then a couple of years ago they went for a short vacation, drove off and were gone about three weeks. When they came back, they didn't go to the Bible Fellowship any more. They clammed up. Went about their business like before, but they'd changed."

Du Pré rolled a smoke.

"From time to time visitors would show up. They wouldn't stay long, and other'n being polite, they didn't have much to say."

Du Pré lit his cigarette.

"Last summer," said Harvey, "they had a sort of conference here, and everybody camped out in the back forty there on the ranch. Lots of traffic in and out. But again, the people who showed up were polite and opaque."

Du Pré nodded.

"All seven of the victims were here," said Harvey.

Du Pré looked at him.

"Something happen then," said Du Pré.

Harvey nodded.

"Thought you should know," he said.

Harvey sauntered on, still staring at the ground.

He turned.

"Every time," he said, "you're gonna do something, you talk Indian more."

Du Pré laughed.

Harvey grinned.

"The Host was most helpful to the agents from the Butte

office," said Harvey, "who of course found nothing whatever. But I wonder just what it was that seven men saw out there that changed their minds and made them leave."

Du Pré nodded.

"Well," said Harvey, "back to my computers. Wonderful things, computers. Tell me things I never wanted to know at all."

Du Pré finished his cigarette and stomped it out and went into the saloon.

Madelaine was reading a magazine.

She looked up at Du Pré.

"You watch out," she said.

Du Pré sat on a stool.

"I got to," he said, "I am around you, my grandkids."

"*Non*," said Madelaine, "that Harvey, that Ripper. They are pissed off, can't do nothing. So they think, well, Du Pré, he will do it for us, we sit back, watch. So, me, I do not know what you are thinking of, but you are not doing it."

"I go on the ranch," said Du Pré. "I look and see about that mine maybe."

Madelaine looked at him, eyes flashing.

"*Non*," she said, "they will be waiting for you. That goddamned Harvey, the son of a bitch he will have to think, something else."

"You want me, sit on my ass?" said Du Pré.

"How 'bout I knock you on it then?" said Madelaine.

Du Pré sighed. He rolled a smoke and lit it and Madelaine took it for her one long drag.

"You never tell me like this before," said Du Pré.

"I don't feel like this before," said Madelaine.

"OK," said Du Pré, "so you tell me some better."

"They got something there, that ranch," said Madelaine. "FBI, cops, they can't go there, they don't know what. They are stuck. You go there it is illegal, you pull some bullshit, blow everything up, it is fine for them. But them Host, they are not fools, Du Pré, they will be waiting you, somebody."

Du Pré nodded.

"I don't get these feelings so much," said Madelaine. "I do, you pay some attention."

Du Pré looked down at his hands.

A year after they had started loving each other, Madelaine and Du Pré had gone up to Canada, on a long driving trip to see relatives. One distant cousin of Du Pré's had built an airplane from a kit, and he had flown it for several hundred hours. He offered to take Du Pré up in it and Du Pré agreed.

Madelaine wouldn't let Du Pré go, and she told the pilot the next time he flew it he would die.

Du Pré's distant cousin laughed at her, called her a foolish woman, and he got in his plane right then and he took off. He was a hundred feet up in the air when the fuel tank exploded.

"OK," said Du Pré, "maybe I go later."

Madelaine nodded.

The door opened and a middle-aged couple came in, pale and shaking, and the man seated his wife and then he came to the bar.

"Two brandies," he said, "if we might."

Madelaine found a couple of snifters and she put shots of brandy in them and the man paid and then he took the big glasses to the table where his wife was sitting.

She was staring off in the distance, and she did not seem to notice when the man set the glass in front of her. He touched her shoulder very gently.

She burst into tears, and she crumpled.

"Why?" she said. "They wouldn't even let us see them."

"Them," said Madelaine, "they are the parents, that woman kill herself, came to see the grandkids."

Du Pré nodded.

"They stop here this morning?" said Du Pré.

Madelaine shook her head.

CHAPTER
27

"He is some good," said Bassman. He lightly tapped the young man on the shoulder with his fist. The young man blushed and looked down at the floor.

It was Friday night. Bassman had driven down from Turtle Mountain with the young accordion player. If you mixed up Bassman and a burlap blonde you might come up with the fella.

"Good," said Du Pré.

The young man held his accordion tightly.

"He is my son," said Bassman.

The boy blushed again.

"I am sitting, my house," said Bassman, "knock at my door. I think what is this, the police again. I open the door. Young Jean-Baptiste, he is standing there. He look at me. He say, 'My mama tell me, you gonna play that damn music all the time, you go find that worthless bastard of a father of yours. Here is the money, get a bus ticket.' So I say, 'Play something.' So he play and it is very good mostly. So I say, 'Which one is your mama?' He say, 'Marcie.' I say that is nice, which one of them, there were two."

Du Pré roared.

"Him say, 'Non, Papa, there were three. I am the one from the one had that big turquoise Cadillac.' So I say, 'Oh, her it is, yes, and I pray she is doing very well a long way, Turtle Mountain.' He say, 'She say, "Tell that fat prick, hope his dick has rotted off." ' I say, 'Yah, her I remember real good, she stab me once.' He say, 'Look, maybe we play some good music, not talk of your women problems which are not mine.' So I say, 'You come on in, have a joint, we see about things.' "

Du Pré and the young man were laughing so hard that people turned to look at them.

"Good you are here," said Du Pré. "You maybe keep Bassman out of some trouble."

Jean-Baptiste shook his head.

"Me," he said, "I just want, play that good music, get in trouble like my papa."

"That is my boy," said Bassman, beaming.

Bassman grinned and went out the back door to find a quiet place to smoke his weed.

"My mama," said Jean-Baptiste, "she say I am a pret' good musician and she feel sorry for all the girls, but she still love Bassman. First time I see him is two days ago, I show up at his house. He tell me he is a real good bass player but not a good father. I tell him we see about that. He is a great guy."

Du Pré nodded.

"Funny," said Jean-Baptiste, "it is like he expects me, be mad at him and I am not."

Du Pré nodded and he rolled a smoke.

"Bassman got a big heart," said Du Pré, "and he play music that is him. He knows you are his son don't want to fuck up."

"He does not," said Jean-Baptiste. "Fuck up would be say,

me, I do not know what you are talking about, slam the door in my face."

"He would not do that, you," said Du Pré. "He is nervous, he will get over it."

"Me, too," said Jean-Baptiste. "I gotta play with you here tonight. Gabriel Du Pré, I got all your tapes, listen to them, listen to my father on them. I don't know I am good enough."

"I don't know," said Du Pré, "*we* are good enough. Tapes are perfect but we are not. Bassman, me, we play so long we know what the other is thinking. You get lost, stop, you find the music, start. There is all that we do."

Jean-Baptiste nodded.

"I go and find my papa," he said. He went out the back door.

The Toussaint Saloon was packed with people and Madelaine and Susan Klein were shoving beers and drinks over the bartop. They worked like demons on Fridays when there was music, serving prime rib, fish, and steaks from five until eight and then clearing the dinner things away so the music could start at nine-thirty.

Du Pré went to the end of the bar where his glass was and reached over and got the bourbon and poured a dram in his glass. He put the bottle back in the rack, dipped up some ice with his hand, and put it in the glass, and then he walked out the back door. It was light yet and only Venus shone in the sky.

Bassman and his son were standing off near some Siberian elms, passing a joint the size of a panetela back and forth.

Du Pré rubbed his hands. They hurt.

The arthritis just like Catfoot had, he is my age now, Du Pré thought, getting old.

Du Pré rolled a smoke and then he lit it and yawned.

He looked over at Bassman and his son.

Jean-Baptiste was pointing to the south.

Du Pré looked up.

Venus was moving and now it had some red in the lights, too.

Du Pré turned to look straight at it.

It moved fast, but not as fast as an airplane.

The lights got closer and Du Pré could hear jet engines.

"Du Pré," shouted Harvey. "Come on! Come on!" He waved as he ran.

Du Pré drained his drink and set the glass on the front boardwalk of the saloon as he passed.

Harvey and Ripper were across the road moving out to the little airstrip. There are some breeze and the windsock flapped.

Du Pré caught up to them.

They were both wearing flak jackets and carrying machine pistols.

"Got my extras," said Ripper. "Ten."

"Check," said Harvey.

The lights were fairly close now.

It was a helicopter with jet engines on it.

The pilot slowed and stopped and then he came straight down and doors opened in the side. Du Pré and Harvey and Ripper ran for them and they got in and pulled the doors to and the helicopter rose and turned and the jet engines screamed and they headed south and west.

"You got a gun?" said Harvey.

Du Pré shook his head.

"Good," said Harvey. "I'd a had to take it away from you. Throw it out."

"What is this?" said Du Pré.

"An hour ago," said Harvey, "McPhie, that big Highway Patrolman, was sitting on the side of the road. Two vehicles passed him, one of 'em had a taillight out.

"Ordinarily he would have let it go, but it was a slow night, and he thought he'd give 'em a warning ticket. So off he goes, gumball machine flashing. The van and the truck pull over, which makes McPhie a little nervous, because he's only after

160

the truck. He is about to get out and do the long walk up there when some little voice says, this is no good. So he flicks on his loudspeaker and he orders everyone out of the vehicles."

Harvey adjusted a strap on his flak jacket.

"McPhie did three tours in Nam and he has real sensitive antennae. Nobody moves up there. He hadn't switched his engine off. He puts the car in reverse and punches it and shoots back. Good thing, too, because right then the rear door of the truck flies up and a whole lotta lead is coming his way. He hunkers down and keeps backing up at seventy, right over the hill. He stops and hollers into the radio. There's a bunch of rocks near the road so he grabs all the guns he's got and he makes a dash and gets there just as the van comes over the hill, guns outta every window."

Du Pré nodded.

"They shoot the shit outta his cruiser and then they get out. McPhie was a grunt and he knows cover. He's got his portable radio. He describes the shooters. He tells the dispatcher where he is exactly. He has time for a couple of crossword puzzles before the people shooting go to the car, which is pretty holed up. They're all women. They aren't soldiers or they would have rushed it right off. Now they know he's got away, so he stands up for a moment and sends off some buckshot and then he ducks down."

"It is them?" said Du Pré.

Harvey looked at him.

"Has to be," he said. "Pidgeon always said the shooters who killed the seven guys were women. Who the hell else could it be?"

Du Pré nodded.

"We're there," said a voice on the intercom.

The helicopter descended rapidly and then it jerked and roared and rose again.

"Shit," said the pilot, "we got hit."

They waited.

"Just some dents," said the pilot. "Everything's fine. But I think I will set you fellers down a little farther away from the festivities."

"Har de har har," said Ripper.

CHAPTER 28

Du Pré and Harvey hunkered down behind a county sheriff's cruiser, and they stared at the two vehicles in the barrow pit. The truck and the van were pulled together, front ends on the rise beyond the deepest portion of the drainage ditch.

There were forty men ringing the two vehicles, all pointing rifles and all with their eyes clapped to telescopic sights. Half of them were sheriff's deputies and half were local people.

"Nothing for a half-hour," said the deputy behind the next car over. "They shot and we shot back. Quite a little firefight. Then it died away and I ain't seen nobody move in there."

"Anybody get a count?" said Harvey.

"Yeah," said the deputy. "McPhie said there was eleven of 'em. Said that was what he saw, hell, there could be more in that truck."

The high rectangular box of the truck was spackled with bullet holes.

"We need an armored car," said Harvey.

"Wal," said the deputy, "few minutes ol' Bender'll be here with his Cat. It's a D-9. We figure we can hide behind the blade and get good and close."

Du Pré laughed.

"Hilarity," said Harvey. "How nice."

"They are all dead," said Du Pré. "You come on now."

He stood and walked up to the macadam and strode down toward the vehicles.

Ripper fell in behind him and then trotted to catch up.

Harvey stood.

Du Pré got close to the truck and went down into the barrow pit.

There were four bodies there, all women, all shot in the head. Du Pré opened the cab of the truck.

Two more.

Ripper danced up to the van and looked down and then he got down on his knees and hands.

He slid open the van's side door.

A woman's body fell halfway out.

She had been blond, and perhaps pretty, but the top of her head was gone and blood and brains dripped from her hollowed skull.

Men came.

"My God," said one. "This is hell."

Harvey was up in the truck box.

He looked around, pointing a flashlight.

"Get an ambulance," he screamed. "Hurry the fuck up."

"Nothin' to do but wait for the coroner," said a deputy. "Where is Larry anyway?"

Ripper leaped into the back of the truck to help Harvey.

Du Pré moved away from the back of the truck. There were a lot of people coming, curious.

An ambulance came up, fast.

The two attendants jumped out, dressed in jeans and boots and the bright shirts of cowboys. They got a wheeled stretcher from the back of their van and brought it to the truck.

The two ambulance attendants got in, both with medical kits.

" 'Bout everybody in the county over fifteen's an EMT," said a deputy. "No way we can afford a hospital."

Harvey leaped from the back of the truck and ran down the road to the helicopter. He stuck his head in the door and then pulled away. The helicopter engines wound up and the jet turbines whined and the helicopter moved slowly up the blacktop and stopped fifty feet from the truck.

The stretcher was slid to the end of the truck bed and the attendants grabbed it and ran toward the helicopter.

Ripper was right behind. He dropped his vest and machine pistol at Du Pré's feet. The stretcher was slid into the helicopter and Ripper got in and slammed the sliding door. The helicopter's engines screamed and the rotors began to whirl. It rose up five hundred feet and then the pilot kicked in the jets and he headed toward Billings. The aircraft was over the horizon in no time.

Du Pré turned and saw McPhie and Harvey and a tall heavy man talking.

County sheriff.

Du Pré knew him. An odd name. Grotbo. One of the Hunkies who had come here to homestead.

Du Pré walked over to them.

" 'Lo, Gabe," said Sheriff Grotbo. "You vouch for this feller?" He nodded at Harvey.

Du Pré shook his head.

"Federal prick," he said.

McPhie and Grotbo and Harvey all laughed.

"You OK?" said Du Pré to McPhie.

McPhie nodded.

"Scared shitless," he said, "but I been that some in my life. Jesus, these people. One shootin' herself is enough, but eleven of 'em?"

"Twelve," said Harvey. "One's still alive, though."

"I can't figure," said McPhie, "what they think they're doin'."

Sheriff Grotbo looked at Du Pré.

"Ain't you supposed to be a-playin' tonight," he said. "Wife said, so we thought we might come give a listen."

Du Pré shrugged.

"You need a rig," said Grotbo, "take mine. Hell, I can ride with Dick."

He held out the keys to his cruiser.

Du Pré looked at Harvey.

"I have a team on the way," said Harvey, "medical examiner, criminal investigation specialists. This is gonna take a long time."

Du Pré nodded. He took the keys.

"Maybe next time," said Grotbo. "Tell you what, tomorrow you get somebody to follow you, drop that in Cooper. I got to come talk to Benny anyway."

Du Pré nodded.

He walked to the cruiser and drove slowly past the mess and the bodies.

He opened it up and headed north and found the road deserted. It was still light.

He looked at his watch.

The helicopter had set down just twenty minutes ago.

Thirty miles down the road he stopped at a roadhouse and got a fifth of bourbon and a plastic glass and ice.

He drove on, the cruiser was new, and it handled very well. The road was utterly empty and for stretches of twenty miles he could see it all.

The cruiser topped at one hundred thirty-two.

Du Pré settled back to one-ten and kept on.

The sun was setting in red glory.

Du Pré got to the crossroads and turned east. He shot along and soon came to Toussaint. He parked across the road from the saloon because every place near the building was taken.

Du Pré got out and stretched. He yawned.

There was music coming from inside.

Bassman and his son. Bassman was playing well. Jean-Baptiste was playing his accordion and singing. He had a good voice, a rich baritone. Du Pré stood out on the front boardwalk smoking and drinking until they were done with their set. Then he went in.

The place was jammed. There were smiling, glistening faces all crowded together. It was very hot. The swamp cooler couldn't pump the heat out from all of the bodies.

People were still whistling and yee-hahing after Bassman and Jean-Baptiste had left the stage.

Jean-Baptiste was so shy he shot out the back door, never looking up from the floor, though people congratulated him as he passed.

Du Pré made his way to the bar. Madelaine and Susan Klein were shoving drinks over and making change at a fast pace.

It would be five minutes or so before Madelaine could stop to even look at Du Pré.

Du Pré went out the back door and glanced over at the Siberian elms. Bassman and Jean-Baptiste were there, smoking weed.

He rubbed the back of his neck.

"What is it, an old man does, get a little wine maybe. A smoke."

Du Pré turned around.

Benetsee was standing there, grinning.

"You got wine, tobacco, your car," said Benetsee, "we go now."

Du Pré looked at him.

Du Pré started to speak.

Benetsee grabbed his arm in his old talons.

"Now," he said.

CHAPTER

29

Benetsee sang.

The air inside Du Pré's cruiser thickened and Du Pré glanced once at the backseat, sure there was someone there. But it was empty. When he looked in the rearview mirror, pale light shimmered like the moon on black water.

Benetsee sang.

Du Pré strained his ears. He could hear singing and drumming, but it was so faint and far he could not be sure.

"Old man!" Du Pré yelled. "What is this? What is this?"

Benetsee sang. When he wanted Du Pré to turn, he snapped his hand out.

"Hah!" said Benetsee. "Stop. Over there. Put this thing over there."

Du Pré followed Benetsee's pointing finger and slid the cruiser into a tiny box canyon between two stumpy buttes.

The old man got out of the cruiser and began to dance in

a circle of whitish dust. Plumes of powdery pale smoke rose from beneath his feet. Benetsee pointed to Du Pré and then to the spot behind his feet, clad in old running shoes and moving faster than an old man could.

Du Pré joined him and Benetsee sang and Du Pré followed, coming in on the chorus.

The chanting and the drums swelled.

There was movement outside the circle just past the light that the eye can see.

Du Pré felt lightheaded.

Benetsee changed to the Blue Jay Dance, and Du Pré followed him.

The chorus of old voices was a soft but solid wall of sound.

Benetsee danced like a blue jay on a tree limb. He cocked his head and ruffled his wings and his feet skittered.

Then he froze.

So did Du Pré.

He smelled rock and dust and caves.

A light beam punched through the dark. It moved toward them and across them. Du Pré could see plastic crates and tubs stacked against rock walls.

"There's nothing here," said a voice.

"That damned sensor's on the fritz again," said another voice. "Said there were two large creatures moving across the beam. Piece of crap."

The light went off.

It was pitch black.

Du Pré cursed silently.

Don't know where I am, old man, what is this?

No. It is that Spanish mine, either the one the badlands or the one the Eide place.

I got no gun, I got no light, I got no fucking idea . . .

Du Pré felt a sharp stab on his cheek and a cold line on the skin.

Blood running.

He breathed deeply.

He stood up.

Little scratchings on the rocky floor of the cave.

Du Pré looked toward the sound.

He saw a pale soft point of light.

It rose and bloomed.

He saw a little blue jay.

Dancing.

The light grew.

The jay danced to a pair of plastic tubs. One of them had its bands cut and the lid was loose. Du Pré lifted it.

Blocks of plastic explosive.

Du Pré pulled out four of them.

The jay jumped up to a shelf.

Du Pré took blasting cord and detonators.

The jay perched on his hand.

Du Pré looked at the cord.

It burned at half a meter per second.

He measured off three and a half meters.

He took a roll of duct tape and he set the blocks of plastic explosive together.

He stuck a detonator in a block and put the end of the blasting cord in the grab socket.

He set the block of explosive on the lip of the bottom plastic crate a foot from the rock wall.

Good baffle and direction, Du Pré thought.

He curled the blasting cord in a spiral on the dry rock floor.

The guards were gone. There was no light and no noise.

Thirty feet to the opening.

Me, I better run faster than that fuse burns.

Du Pré pulled out his shepherd's lighter and picked up the end of the blasting cord.

The flashlight beam came on again and it stabbed into the cave.

"There's no other way *in* there," said a voice, "and we've been right here."

"I checked the sensors," said the other voice, "switched it off and on and it tells me there's a man in here, god damn it."

"Blasphemy is a sin, brother," said the other voice.

"I am going to take a look," said the voice.

Du Pré sank down behind the crates. He kept the fuse and the lighter in his hand.

The beam from the flashlight played around the cave and stopped.

Three steps on the rocky floor.

The beam went over Du Pré's head.

"There isn't anyone there," said the voice outside the cave.

"Thoroughness is grace in the Eyes of Yahweh," said the voice near Du Pré.

Du Pré rasped the lighter and it caught and he touched the glowing end of the rope to the fuse. There was a spark and a faint hiss.

Du Pré looked up at the ceiling.

He set the fuse down and it burned rapidly around the spiral.

He stood up.

A man was standing fifteen feet from him, looking off to the side where the flashlight beam played.

Du Pré yelled and he ran for the entrance. His voice filled the chamber.

He went through the entrance, a racket of whaps hitting the stone walls behind him.

There was a stand of small trees to the left.

Du Pré dived behind them and he scrambled forward on his hands and knees. He went behind a slab of rock.

"It's just a fucking coyote," said the voice outside the cave. "A damned—"

The explosion came in two parts, a crump and then a blast as the gasses blew out the door of the cave.

Du Pré kept flat, his hands over his head. His ears filled and he was deaf. The stink of explosives choked him.

Rocks began to fall.

Du Pré stood up.

He looked at the cave.

It wasn't there. A cloud of dust hung where the entrance had been.

A body lay broken fifty feet away. Du Pré went over to it. He looked under it. There was the stock of a rifle.

Kalashnikov. Du Pré pulled back the slide, and brass gleamed.

These fuckers they work, they got dirt, ice, epoxy in them, Du Pré thought.

He trotted off toward the badlands. They hung in the air. Ground fog lay in a thin cloud over the prairie.

On the Eide ranch then, my car is . . .

Du Pré turned. His ears were thick and ringing.

Lights danced.

Headlamps, ORVs, trucks, all racing toward the old mine.

Du Pré spat. His mouth was full of pulverized rock and his nostrils burned.

He trotted on.

A fence. Du Pré moved toward it.

There were huge dark boulders on the earth.

They moved.

Buffalo. Hundreds of them. They began to move together.

A huge bull snorted and pawed the earth.

Du Pré nodded to the bull as he passed.

Good evening, my brother.

He stepped through the fence.

A noisemaker on top of a fencepost began to shriek.

CHAPTER
30

Du Pré stopped as soon as he got into the badlands. He looked down at his feet.

Moccasins.

He shook his head.

Me, I do not remember putting these on.

He was terribly thirsty. He found a pebble the size of a cherry and put it in his mouth.

There were several trails braiding through the badlands.

My car . . . I am not sure where it is.

"You old shit!" yelled Du Pré. "We fly there I got to walk back."

A small engine screamed back toward the fence he had stepped through.

Du Pré picked a track that led into a narrow defile cut into the soft stone. He trotted along.

Old son of a bitch, he thought, this time maybe you get me killed, arrested maybe.

Engines screamed.

Du Pré came out of the narrow slit in the rock and he saw another across the pan, perhaps a hundred yards away. He ran for it, leaping over a small gully in the middle, cut by the rain that so seldom fell. The wind rose up. He dived into the slit in the wall of rock.

He stopped and turned. It was so narrow he had to swing the assault rifle down toward the ground to point it back toward the pan.

Lights bounced a half mile up the wide track.

Seven sets.

The wind suddenly kicked up ferociously. Screams and moans rose from the *malpais*. Clouds of dust raced thick toward the lights coming on.

Du Pré smelled water.

Rain.

He looked up.

The day had been cloudless. Now it was black, and lightning flashed inside the heavy clouds, edging them with purple and gold and white.

Du Pré backed into the slit. It twisted and turned and the walls rose higher and higher.

Me, I do not like this, I am getting deeper in the earth.

Du Pré went on. The slit narrowed.

"In here!" someone yelled. "Fresh tracks!"

A burst of automatic fire. Du Pré dropped down. Richochets whined and whirred and screamed.

Shoot me like a skunk in a culvert.

Du Pré rose and he moved on.

There was a chimney in the rock, a square narrow cut up to the rim. Du Pré ripped the sleeves from his shirt. He tied them together and he looped the cloth around the pistol grip of the Kalashnikov. He tied off the loop and the ends, then put it around his neck so that the rifle hung down straight. He slid into the chimney and put his back against the rock and his hands and knees against the other side.

He began to inch his way up.

Another burst of automatic weapon fire. The slugs screamed down the slit where he had been.

It was easier going than he had feared. The width of the chimney was perfect. He felt with his toes and found a foothold. He stuck his foot in it. Secure, he ran his fingers over the rock face.

Holes.

Somebody cut me a staircase.

He stepped up, a couple feet at a time now.

More gunfire. A slug hit the rock near his right hand and splinters of stone sprayed him.

Du Pré moved up.

Rain.

Huge drops. Just a few, but when they hit they went *splack*!

The rim was six feet above him. Du Pré inched up to it. He slowly lifted his head and looked carefully around the misshapen cap of stone.

No one.

Du Pré crawled up and out. He made for a deep shadow under a ledge of stone.

The skies opened. Du Pré shoved his body as far under the ledge as it could go. Hailstones crashed on the rocks, and bits of ice splattered Du Pré's face. The rain came down in a torrent. Rills of water ran under the ledge, icy and swift.

Du Pré blinked.

Old fucker, I think I maybe just shoot you I find you.

Save my ass so I drown.

Ver' funny.

The water was standing two inches deep on every surface but the steepest, and there were pools of water, dark and frothy, pounded to foam by the relentless rain.

The rain stopped.

Lightning flashed.

Du Pré crawled out from under the ledge and looked around. The water was running rapidly off the cap. Stone appeared, and then the pools in the hollows sank as the water sought the lowest place.

Du Pré stood up. He stepped away from the ledge and he looked very carefully around.

Nothing moved.

Shadows.

Stones.

Water.

Du Pré moved quickly toward the edge of the cap, where he thought the slit he had gone into began. His moccasins held to the rock. They almost felt sticky.

Du Pré went down on his belly and edged toward the lip and at an inch a minute he poked his head out. Then he turned his eyes side to side.

Waters roiled, thick with mud.

Du Pré looked at the rocks below.

A man sat there, shivering. He held a light assault rifle. The man was looking around, slowly.

"Above you, Mike!" someone screamed.

Du Pré jerked his head back and rolled to a dip in the stone. An automatic rifle ripped and slugs whacked into the lip of the cap of rock. Some went right overhead, going *crack*!

Du Pré wriggled backward, and then he stood and ran for the far, north end of the capstone. He jumped over a few shallow small pools. Looking down, he saw the stars reflected in one. He got to the edge and fell on his belly and wriggled to the lip and looked down.

The waters were sinking into the earth.

"Over here!" someone shouted, back toward the other side of the rock.

Du Pré swung his legs over the lip and slid down, holding

the rifle high overhead. The scarp wasn't steep and it was very wet. Du Pré left only a little skin on it. His feet hit the pavement stones at the bottom and he crouched and turned.

No one was there.

Du Pré ran across the watercourse. There was another narrow slit in the rock. He went into the deep shadow. The cleft went through and out the other side. Across another wide flat pan there was another cleft. Du Pré dashed for it.

A helicopter whacked overhead, a searchlight stabbed down from it. Du Pré trotted through the cleft, a good four feet wide. The helicopter moved off to the south. Du Pré splashed through a pool of water. He went out the other side of the stone.

Du Pré stopped.

His cruiser was sitting there. A cigarette glowed in the front. Du Pré walked to the car and got in.

"You don't dance so good," said Benetsee. "Here, have something to drink."

CHAPTER
31

Du Pré parked in the tall grass near Benetsee's cabin. The old man had sung on the drive home, his head hanging, his cracked voice gathering strength and then fading away. The words were in a language Du Pré didn't know.

Du Pré thought that he had heard drumming, but then it could have been the tires on the road.

They sat in the car and Benetsee sang.

The old man stopped and raised his head and grinned. He held up his hand. There was a deep gash across the back of it, and Du Pré could see tendons white against the dark red wound.

"I take you to the doctor," said Du Pré. He reached for the key in the ignition.

Benetsee laughed.

"Needs new flesh," he said. "Me, I will take care of it."

Benetsee opened the door and got out, yawned and shook himself. He went to the cabin door.

Pelon opened it. The cabin had been dark.

Du Pré got out. He reached under the seat for his plastic flask of whiskey. He had some and rolled a smoke and another for the old man. He lit both of them and walked to the cabin and up the two steps to the sagging porch. Pelon opened the door again. The night was cold, but inside the cabin it was warm. A fire raged in the old woodstove, the flames danced behind the isinglass windows in the door.

Benetsee sat at the little table. He had a basin of water and a rag and he bathed his wound and he sang.

He put his fingers into a steer's horn bottle and got a gob of dark jam. He smeared this on the wound and he sang.

Pelon lit a small twist of sweetgrass and the smoke curled up, pungent and holy.

"One of them big Band-Aids," said Benetsee. Pelon got a huge one from a first aid kit under a badger's skin. He peeled away the paper wrapping and took the plastic covers from the stickum and put the big patch over Benetsee's hand.

"Whiteman's Band-Aids, duct tape," said Benetsee, "they don't do much right, but them I like."

Du Pré laughed. He went to the table and picked up the steer's horn bottle. He smelled the paste.

Balsam of Peru.

He looked at the horn. It was old and badly cracked. There was a metal band around it, with a ring on one side. The stopper was new, carved of dry cottonwood. Du Pré put the stopper in and set the horn back on the table.

Benetsee smiled. Then he put his head down on the table. He snored.

Du Pré and Pelon went outside. They looked off toward the east. Helicopters were circling something, their red and green running lights winking many miles away.

"Strobes," said Pelon. "Got some candlepower."

Du Pré rolled two smokes and gave one to Pelon.

"We go, that ranch," said Du Pré. "Me, I do not know how."

Pelon laughed.

"Yah," he said, "I watch you. You dance pret' good. Dance like the blue jay."

Du Pré looked at him. Pelon grinned.

"I was sweating for you, singing," he said.

Du Pré nodded.

A car was coming up the county road, fast. The sound of the engine carried far in the empty night.

Pelon looked at Du Pré.

"We sweat, sing tonight," he said.

Du Pré nodded.

"Sweat a long time."

Du Pré nodded.

"Them Host of Yahweh," said Pelon, "they are in some big trouble now. Got no place to run to, them. Big fight. You don't get killed maybe."

Du Pré shrugged.

"Come," said Pelon, "we put the old man to bed. They will be here in a minute. Him, he need sleep."

They went inside and picked up Benetsee and they carried him out of the door and down past the sweat lodge. There was a bedroll hidden in the willows and alders by the creek. They put Benetsee in it. The old man smelled of woodsmoke, wine, tobacco, and balsam of Peru.

"Him maybe don't want to talk, them," said Pelon. "He want to change and hide, him can."

Pelon's Coyote French was getting much better, Du Pré thought.

He looked older, too. All of the city fat was gone.

"What he do now?" said Du Pré.

Pelon laughed.

"Nothing we think of," he said. "Him, he will make his joke. Always does. Us, we get to be punch lines."

Du Pré nodded.

"Benetsee is not there," said Du Pré, "so how is he hurt?"

Pelon laughed.

"Slapping something away," said Pelon, "you maybe itch someplace?"

Du Pré looked at him. He did itch, just to the right of the bottom of his left shoulder blade.

Just above my heart.

"Jesus," said Du Pré.

"He is old," said Pelon. "Makes him tired, that."

Du Pré blew out smoke.

The car was getting near. A cruiser. The light bar was flashing. No siren.

"We sweat," said Pelon.

Du Pré nodded.

The lights flashed and blinked and the car turned in to the track that led up to the cabin. Benny Klein's cruiser. The car came to a stop and both doors opened. Benny stood up slowly. Ripper shot out and began to run to Du Pré and Pelon.

Ripper stopped. He danced a little on his feet.

"Where the hell you been? As if I didn't know," he said.

"Long sweat here," said Du Pré. "We just stop, hour ago maybe."

Ripper looked at him.

He walked over to Du Pré's cruiser and put his hand on the hood.

"Cold, Benny," said Ripper. "Hasn't been run for six hours at least."

"That's good," said Benny.

"Knew you'd like it," said Ripper. "Now, somebody blew up a cache on the Host of Yahweh ranch. Blew it up good. Killed two people, we can tell ya, and scattered parts of ordnance for quite a ways. Heard the racket in town, we did, and so out we went. Know what happened? We were told we couldn't come in, take a look."

Du Pré nodded.

"So," said Ripper, "I said we goddamn well would as large explosions were de facto evidence of large explosives which are illegal to possess."

Du Pré nodded.

"Standoff for a while," said Ripper.

Benny was chewing some snoose. He spat.

"Now," said Ripper, "the guards at the gate were flunks, and they had their orders, and then something extraordinary happened."

Du Pré waited.

He looked over at Benny's cruiser. There was a long crease in the hood, showing black against the white paint.

"They shot at us," said Ripper, "can you imagine? Now, give 'em credit, they weren't really trying to hit us, I don't think, and so we left."

"Where is Harvey?" said Du Pré.

"He was in Billings," said Ripper, "but he came right back."

Du Pré rolled a smoke.

"So," said Ripper, "Harvey says to me, Ripper, I smell something here. Maybe you would go and ask Du Pré what that smell is."

Du Pré waited.

"And here I am," said Ripper.

Du Pré spread out his hands palm up.

"Right," said Ripper. "Well, Pidgeon is on her way, and I know you would like to stare at her ass."

Du Pré shrugged.

"The troops are arriving by the platoon," said Ripper.

Du Pré shrugged.

"Officer Parker is in there," said Ripper, "and that's a story all by itself."

CHAPTER

32

The Host of Yahweh compound was brightly lit. Every mercury lamp blazed.

No one moved in it.

Harvey Wallace looked grimly at the metal buildings and the partly completed mansion.

"We could," he said, "be here for quite a long time."

Du Pré snorted.

For a long time. After Waco, they don't charge in anymore. That is good.

"Waco," said Harvey. "Monumental stupidity. Sheriff over in western Montana, had one of his deputies killed by some nutbar, guy lived in a fort in the woods, so you know what that sheriff did?"

Du Pré looked at him.

"Waited, what he did," said Harvey. "Told the state police and us ever-helpful feds to please fuck off. Waited the guy out.

Waited a *year and a half,* he did. Finally the bastard got careless, figured his murdering the deputy had been forgotten or something, drove out of his fort to take a little fresh air, and wham, that sheriff got him. No gunfire. No tanks. Nobody killed. Guy, we could use a director. You know him?"

Du Pré shook his head.

"So we may be here a long time," said Harvey. He looked bleakly at the brightly lit compound. "Here in the fucking cactus."

Du Pré laughed.

"Ripper tells me," said Harvey, "that you were peacefully worshipping in the sweat lodge, there at Benetsee's. Engine's cold, so it could not possibly have been you touched off the bang there."

Du Pré nodded.

"I believe everything Ripper tells me," said Harvey. "Thanks anyway. That we got covered. They had enough weapons and explosives in there to kill a whole lot of people."

Du Pré looked at him.

"ATF's all over it," said Harvey. "Got here in a hurry they did. So the arsenal there is blown. Now what, I wonder, have they got in there?"

"Whatever they got," said Ripper, "they got less of it now."

"A good thing," said Harvey, "but I still worry."

"Pidgeon will be here shortly," said Ripper.

"Driving?" said Harvey. Pidgeon drove flat out and so far had fried three government cars Du Pré knew of.

"Flying," said Ripper.

"Well," said Harvey, "it's slower for her, but probably safer."

"Harvey," said Ripper, "you want to move at horseback speed, you got to ride a horse."

"I got a job for you," said Harvey.

"Harvey," said Ripper, "fuck off."

"See?" said Harvey, looking at Du Pré, "this is what happens when you let up. Time was, he prefaced everything with *sir.*"

Suddenly all of the lights in the compound went off.

"They here yet?" said Harvey.

"Nope," said Ripper, "be another couple hours. You know how it is. National Guard, they have to find their searchlights, then find the batteries, takes time."

"So we didn't do that?" said Harvey.

"Nope," said Ripper.

Du Pré looked to the west. A helicopter was headed right for them. Its light stabbed down.

Harvey looked at it.

"That's Pidgeon," said Harvey, "no doubt. You need to click a light at her or something?"

"Nope," said Ripper, "she's on the phone. You wanna talk with her?"

He handed his cell phone to Harvey.

"Hi, gorgeous," Harvey said breathily.

Pidgeon said something and Harvey laughed. He handed the phone back to Ripper.

The helicopter descended on a flat open meadow a hundred yards back from the front gate of the Host of Yahweh ranch.

Pidgeon ducked out of the door and ran crouched over till she was well past the rotors. Two men carrying aluminum cases followed.

Harvey took another look at the dark compound.

Nothing moved.

Du Pré squinted and he looked to the south. There was another helicopter circling far away.

Two dark figures burst out of the shadows near one of the metal Host of Yahweh buildings and they ran to shadows by another and disappeared.

Pidgeon walked up to Harvey, puffing a little.

"Whadda we do now?" said Harvey. "Call in an airstrike?"

Pidgeon ignored him. The men came up behind her.

"You got a commvan for me?" she said.

Harvey nodded and Ripper spoke into his cell phone. An

engine started and a dark van with a satellite dish on it came slowly up. It had been parked back with the cop cars.

"Where are the TV folks?" said Pidgeon.

"Roads are blocked," said Harvey.

"Harvey," said Pidgeon, "I keep tellin' you not to work so hard at pissin' them off."

"For all I know," said Harvey, "the Host may come out shooting. No TV, no reporters, no nothin' till we know a bit more."

Pidgeon nodded.

"Hi, Du Pré," she said. "Long time no see."

Du Pré laughed.

"I'm here, too," said Ripper.

"So you are," said Pidgeon. "Nothing's perfect."

"Pidgeon!" said one of the men in the van. "We got something!"

Pidgeon turned and ran to the van. She got in and slid the door shut.

"Wonders of modern communications," said Harvey.

"Parker, she is in there?" said Du Pré.

Harvey nodded.

"She gets in trouble," said Harvey, "we go in shootin'."

Du Pré sighed.

"Pidgeon's talking with her probably," said Harvey.

Du Pré looked at him.

"Parker got in, hell, we didn't even know it. That woman at the massacre, one was still alive, she still is, but she isn't talking much. How Parker got back here so quick from California we don't know, but she did."

Du Pré sighed.

"Those women shot themselves and each other," said Harvey. "They were the assassins. Had a few trophies, show the White Priest, I suppose. I dunno how that bastard gets people to do this shit, but he does."

"So," said Du Pré. "You wait, why?"

"Waco," said Harvey, "is why. There'll be three hundred

agents here by daylight. Searchlights. We were gonna shut the power off then. Then we wait 'em out."

Du Pré nodded.

"This worries me," said Harvey. "Those fools at Waco weren't all that smart. It was one of those things, happens. These people are a good deal more competent. Very little false front."

"Them women," said Du Pré, "you are sure?"

Harvey nodded.

"Yeah," he said. "Yeah, it was real clear. We don't know much, but it just looks like when the guys wanted to leave, the White Priest said OK, fine, go, no hard feelings. Then he sends the girls, kill 'em all at the same time."

Du Pré shook his head.

"Yeah," said Harvey, "things folks will do when they really believe."

Pidgeon opened the van door and she motioned for Harvey to come. He walked over. Pidgeon and Harvey stood together, heads down, listening. Harvey waved to Du Pré.

Du Pré walked to the van.

The technician fiddled with something.

A voice, weird and distorted.

"Electronic voice cover," said Pidgeon.

"It is not the Last Days," said the voice.

A chorus of Praise Yahwehs.

"Here we must stand," said the voice.

Praise Yahweh.

"The Legions of Arcturus and Betelgeuse are flaming through the stars and they shall succor us."

Praise Yahweh.

"The Assyrians draw nigh our gates."

Praise Yahweh.

"They shall not enter to destroy our Temple."

Praise Yahweh.

"I will go now," said Du Pré.

He walked toward his cruiser.

CHAPTER

33

Du Pré sat at Madelaine's kitchen table. They had just eaten venison saddle with plum sauce and wild rice with little strong onions Madelaine raised in the garden boxes Du Pré had built for her. She had more than seventy herbs and spices in the boxes. One, fifteen feet long, was all chives.

They finished and Du Pré washed the dishes. He dried the silver and put it away in the velvet-lined box.

Catfoot had found the silver, in its chest, in an abandoned wagon he stumbled across in the Wolf Mountains. The wagon had furniture and cast-iron cookware in it, too. There was no sign of who had left it, decades before.

The silverware was heavy and had a crest on it and the initials GP in raised scrolled script.

"Du Pré," Madelaine had said when she had first looked at it, "it is a sign from God. You change your name, Placquemines, it is yours."

"Too many letters," Du Pré had said.

Madelaine made coffee and they took it out back and sat near the double-bloom Persian lilacs. There was a faint scent yet, though the blossoms had long fallen.

"So," said Madelaine, "what is Du Pré going to do?"

Du Pré shrugged.

"Me," he said, "I think I play my fiddle, let them fix that one."

A TV news helicopter whacked over, and it set down in the meadow across from the Toussaint Saloon, a third of a mile away.

"Those children in there," said Madelaine, "they better be thinkin' of them, all the time. Poor kids."

Du Pré nodded.

There was a good three hours of light left.

Horse hooves. A little horse.

Pallas came round the house on her little blue roan. She stepped down and dropped the reins. The horse stood.

"Hi," said Pallas. "I got to talk, you."

Du Pré narrowed his eyes.

This Pallas, he thought, thinks so fast, me I get whiplash tryin' to keep up.

"Bout me marryin' Ripper," said Pallas. "It's a while you know."

Du Pré nodded.

"It's OK he marries somebody else long as he divorces her then," said Pallas.

"You tell him this?" said Madelaine.

Pallas shook her head.

"I thought Grandpère could," she said.

"Me," said Madelaine, "I need more coffee, be right back."

"Ver' generous of you," said Du Pré.

"Don't want Ripper to think I am mean," said Pallas. "Sides, he is prolly pret' horny."

"What happens," said Du Pré, "Ripper don't want to get married, you or anybody?"

"I take care of that," said Pallas.

Madelaine stayed in the house. Du Pré saw her once, looking quickly out the kitchen window and laughing like hell.

"OK," said Du Pré, "I tell him."

"Thanks, Grandpère," said Pallas. She got back on her little blue roan and she turned him and they went.

Madelaine came back out.

"That kid," said Du Pré, "she is scaring me some."

"Good," said Madelaine, "she about scare anybody. Poor Ripper, he think he got a life, he don't, he don't do what she say."

Du Pré nodded. Another TV helicopter went over.

"Them buffalo," said Madelaine, "what they do with them?"

Du Pré looked at her. He shrugged.

"Poor things," said Madelaine. "I hope they got enough water. Grass."

Du Pré hadn't thought about them. They had been let out to the huge back pasture.

"I don't know how much water there is," he said.

Madelaine nodded.

"They pump any, got no electricity," she said. "It is maybe not enough. Who is maybe taking care of that?" said Madelaine.

Du Pré sighed.

"All right," he said. "I go see that Harvey."

Madelaine beamed at him.

"Come down here for them buffalo, our people," she said. "We maybe should see they are all right."

Du Pré got up.

"You maybe tell that Ripper he can get laid, Pallas she give him her gracious permission," said Madelaine.

Du Pré nodded. He yawned and he stretched.

"Horses," said Madelaine. "See about them, too."

The wild horses.

"Me," said Du Pré, "I will go, conserve all that nature."

He walked out to his cruiser. He got in. There was a little box wrapped in white tissue paper on the front seat.

For Ripper, said the card, *from Pallas.*

Du Pré smelled it.

Chocolate chip cookies.

"He is that dead meat," said Du Pré. He turned the key and started the engine and he drove off east and then north.

The armed camp that surrounded the Host of Yahweh compound largely lived in trailers that had been trucked in and hooked up to electricity and water, that last brought in huge tanker trucks. The trailers were out of sight if one looked out from the compound. Men in body armor carrying automatic weapons patrolled a perimeter, some on foot and some in armored personnel carriers.

Du Pré parked where the newsmen did and he walked to the sentry at the gate in the worn fence.

"Me," said Du Pré, "I need to see that Harvey Wallace."

"Certainly, Mr. Du Pré," said the sentry. "Go on in. Fourth trailer on the right."

Du Pré walked on.

He found the trailer and knocked on the door.

A young man opened it. He looked at Du Pré, startled, and his hand reached for the gun in his waistband.

"It's OK, Melton," said Harvey.

The young man relaxed.

"Sorry," he said.

Du Pré shrugged and he went on in. The room stank of sweat, bad coffee, and electrical currents.

Harvey yawned. He looked exhausted.

"They're good," he said. "They have generators and wells and a lot of food. We demand they surrender. They don't reply."

"What about the stock?" said Du Pré.

Harvey looked at him dully.

"Them buffalo," said Du Pré, "they are all right?"

Harvey shook himself.

"I assume," he said, "that they are out there eating grass and humping each other like buffalo."

"Anybody go look?" said Du Pré.

Harvey shook his head.

"Sometimes they come in near the sentries at night," said the young agent. "But there's been no trouble."

"What," said Harvey, "am I supposed to do with the *goddamned buffalo?*"

Du Pré stood and he waited.

"Gabriel," said Harvey, "will you please go and see how those monstrous hairballs are?"

"Sure," said Du Pré.

"Get him a pass," said Harvey, "and then we need to compose a memo."

The young agent took Du Pré's picture, pulled it out of the camera, waited, and then pulled the print apart.

"Driver's license?" said the agent. Du Pré handed it to him.

"Where is Ripper?" said Du Pré.

Harvey yawned.

"I dunno," said Harvey.

Du Pré handed him the box of chocolate chip cookies.

"From his fiancé," said Du Pré.

"I'll see he gets them," said Harvey.

"Here's your pass," said the young agent. "Clip it to your shirt."

Du Pré stuck it on his pocket.

Ripper came in.

"Ripper me boy," said Harvey, waving the box, "come speak with your Dutch uncle."

CHAPTER
34

Du Pré clucked to the big bay and the horse muscled up the cutbank. As soon as the footing was flat, the bay began to trot.

They are around here someplace, Du Pré thought. Strange how a big animal can disappear. Cattle hide but they are not that good at it. Buffalo are very good at it.

He found a water hole, trampled and ruined, the earth and mud churned up and the spring strangled beneath the blackened ground. A few hoofprints had water in the bottom, but not many. The pipe surround that kept the cattle from wrecking the spring was a twisted and trampled mess of bent iron.

My grandpère tell me the time he goes to round up buffalo, over in the Flathead Valley, they got this bison range. They are going to ship buffalo to Canada. They got a hundred cowboys, they got a train with cattle cars on it.

Buffalo don't think much of this. One bull he hooks a horse, horn goes right through the cinch ring, buffalo picks up the horse and rider, carries them half a mile, throws them over a bank. Horse is gutted, intestines dragging on the ground. Cowboys, they try to rope them buffalo. Buffalo, they charge the cowboys. I stuff your rope up your ass, dumb shit.

They haze some buffalo into the cars, the train. The buffalo tear the cars apart.

"Knock them planks to kindling," said grandpère, "kick out the sides, then they jump straight up, land legs all stiff. Chips fly everywhere. Planks are oak. They don't last long."

Foreman has to wire the Canadians.

You want your damn buffalo, you come get them here.

Canadians they wire back, oh, it is all right, we think of something else maybe, you keep your buffalo.

Me, I don't know much about them but old stories.

My people, they eat all of the buffalo Manitoba, Saskatchewan. They come down here to hunt, make meat and pemmican sell to that Hudson's Bay Company. Many many tons. We got guns, we kill them, we run them into traps. Hunt leader is called the Poundmaker, he makes those log corrals, pounds, run them buffalo in, shut the gate and kill them all.

Best meat is the unborn calves.

Du Pré stopped and he looked at the ground. Fresh tracks and shit still damp in the middle. Dry wind, maybe an hour old.

"Where are them sons of bitches, eh?" said Du Pré to his horse.

The horse stood, his ears pointing one place and then another. The land stretched away. Broken and looking very empty. But there were coulees cut by vanished rivers and gullies cut by thunderstorms that dumped a million tons of water on a small patch of the earth, the lottery of rain in this country.

Du Pré cantered over to a low butte and he let the horse pick its way up a narrow trail to the top. He stopped and he looked around. The land looked soft, gray and green and lavender. There was grass eaten down to the ground.

Not a buffalo in sight.

Du Pré laughed.

Flying over the place he had looked down and seen them black and rounded, like raisins in an oatmeal earth. There were thousands in here, over three, and they had disappeared.

Du Pré rode to the edge of the butte and looked down.

A buffalo bull stood in the coulee below him. The huge animal was barely forty feet away.

The bull was motionless.

Nothing moved but a jay picking bugs from the black-brown cape of thick and twisted hair covering the buffalo's huge shoulders.

Du Pré looked at the massive beast.

The buffalo did not twitch. The bird hopped on its back, pecking. The buffalo's short skinny tail flicked once.

"You see me, eh?" said Du Pré.

The tail whirled around. The clump of hair at the end flapped. The buffalo snorted. Du Pré's horse had started to tremble.

"Ho ho ho," said Du Pré, rubbing the bay's neck.

The tail hung motionless. Then it began to whirl again.

The buffalo's round black eye stared. A cloud of little flies danced around it but the eye did not blink. The horse danced a little and he snorted.

"Easy, easy," said Du Pré. The edge of the low butte fell away almost sheer, a good twenty feet.

Du Pré rolled a smoke and he lit it and he looked up.

A helicopter was circling the Host of Yahweh compound.

"Them TV," said Du Pré to the horse.

The buffalo was motionless again. The jay hopped to a new spot and it pecked.

Long damn way from a tree that jay is, Du Pré thought.

The horse whinnied. The bay was nervous and trembling. The helicopter rose up and it hung in the air for a moment and then it turned toward Du Pré and it began to come on.

Son of a bitch. What they are doing this for, thought Du Pré.

He stared at the helicopter, getting a little larger as it came on. The horse backed a little and it snorted and shook its head.

"Easy," said Du Pré.

The buffalo's trail whirled. It stopped, sticking up and out. The buffalo lifted its right front leg and it pawed the ground. It bellowed once and it spun on its front legs and it charged the rock wall.

The horse reared and Du Pré dropped his cigarette and he grabbed the reins.

"Whoa, you son of a bitch," yelled Du Pré.

Du Pré clamped his legs tight. The horse turned and bolted for the trail they had come up on. Du Pré pulled back on the reins.

The horse ignored him. They sailed off the lip of the butte and landed on the pan. The horse took the shock and then it bounded ahead. The trail was fairly open and Du Pré stood in the stirrups, trying to turn the horse.

He heard the buffalo bull below and behind him.

Du Pré turned, eyes wide.

The bull sailed off the lip of the butte. Du Pré turned and put his head near the horse's neck and dug his heels into the bay's flanks.

"You," said Du Pré to the horse, "run all you want to."

The horse was going flat out, galloping across the water-carved pan and then leaping a low bank to shortgrass prairie.

Du Pré looked back.

The huge bull was thundering along behind them, and it was closer.

Jesus, Du Pré thought, that bastard wants to kill us.

He could not come up that rock wall.

Son of a bitch did, though.

The ground rolled away and the bay stretched out. They ran a good mile, and when Du Pré glanced back the bull buffalo was well behind, and had lost a hundred yards on the horse.

Du Pré looked ahead.

This horse it will be blown here another couple miles.

OK.

He looked back again. The huge bull was closer. They came over a rise and Du Pré looked ahead in horror.

Hundreds of buffalo were scattered over the ground, some grazing, some lying down. Reddish calves capered.

The horse plunged on. The buffalo stirred and the lying ones stood up. Du Pré and his bay got to them and the bay shot between two groups. Then the buffalo ran. One instant they were still and the next they were running full speed.

Hail Mary and God damn it, Du Pré thought.

The horse dropped down into a hidden cleft in the land. Buffalo stood thick in it. They threw up their tails and they ran.

Du Pré and the bay were galloping in the middle of the herd. The huge animals pounded the ground, which drummed.

Du Pré looked ahead.

The heavy fence the Host had spent millions of dollars on was a half mile away. The buffalo pounded on.

Du Pré tried to rein in his horse. The big bay stumbled and Du Pré fell and he rolled twenty feet.

He looked up. The buffalo were coming at him. They passed by him, going to the sides. He closed his eyes.

He heard the wires break, a sound like one of the strings on his violin failing, but deeper and louder.

The dust was thick. The buffalo were gone.

Du Pré stood up. The helicopter thwacked overhead. Du Pré looked at the TV camera poking out the side door.

He gave it the finger.

CHAPTER

35

"Well," said Madelaine, "you got them buffalo all organized."

They were watching the evening news. The footage of the buffalo stampede with Du Pré bouncing along in the middle of it had run for a good minute. Then there was the shot of the buffalo running into the fence. One animal hit the wires, which all parted, and that bull did not flinch or break stride.

Du Pré felt his ribs. He had landed on a rock with some of them and they hurt. His elbow was raw. He had cactus spines in his right thigh.

He took a good swallow of bourbon.

"A sight few today may see," said the announcer.

More footage of the buffalo racing through the badlands. They broke into streams when the land cut close and they became a brown river when it opened up.

"The Old West still lives," said the announcer.

"God dang," said Booger Tom, "musta been downright excitin'. Now you are tellin' me this bull just bounded up a twenty-foot cliff and took off after you?"

Du Pré nodded.

"Whaddya do to piss him off?" said Booger Tom.

"Tell him one of your jokes," said Du Pré.

"Which one?" said the old cowboy.

Du Pré nodded.

The door to the saloon opened and Bart came in. He was grinning evilly.

"HOME, HOME ON THE RAAAAAAAAAAAAAANGE . . ." he bellowed.

Du Pré held his glass out to Madelaine. She put whiskey in it. She patted his hand.

"They wear out soon," she said.

Du Pré nodded.

"Pretty good fall you did there," said Booger Tom. "When I was in the moving picture business I recall a fall like that'd get ya a ten-dollar bonus . . . Course, we made a point of knowin' where the *cactus* was."

Du Pré nodded.

"Well," said Bart, "thank God you're all right."

Du Pré looked at him.

"Me, I am not all right."

"What?" said Bart.

"His friends," said Madelaine. "Du Pré survives a buffalo stampede, that is the easy part, then he has got to live past his friends."

"HOME, HOME ON THE RAAAAAAAAAAAA-ANNNNNNNNNGGGGGGGGGE," bellowed Bart and Booger Tom.

"Old man," said Madelaine, "your voice it sounds like goat farts in a tin shed."

"Give me a beer," said Booger Tom, "without the music criticism."

Du Pré dug at a mess of cactus spines in his elbow with the point of his knife.

"They'll fester out," said Booger Tom.

"So will his friends," said Madelaine.

Booger Tom sipped his beer.

Bart sipped his soda.

The front door banged open. Du Pré turned to look.

It was Jacqueline. She was angry, flamingly furious.

She looked around the room.

"You see that Pallas?" said Jacqueline.

Everybody shook their head.

Jacqueline went back out, slamming the door.

"Uh-oh," said Bart.

Du Pré shrugged.

You have them kids, they drive you nuts, Du Pré thought, thing that they got to do, like eat.

"Me," said Madelaine, "I never see that Jacqueline so mad. Maybe you better go and see about it."

Du Pré nodded.

"Need help?" said Booger Tom, eyes wide and innocent.

Du Pré looked at him for a long moment, then shook his head.

Du Pré went back out.

Jacqueline was stomping up the street, peering in yards. She went up to a house and banged on the door. It opened and she said something to Mrs. La Barge and then Jacqueline left and headed on.

The van was parked there. Some kids were sitting in it. Du Pré went to the van. He slid open the door.

The children were sitting very quietly, looking at the hands in their laps.

"OK," said Du Pré, "me, I never see your mother so angry. What is it? She is mad at Pallas."

Looks.

"We don't know," said Berne.

"Yeah," said Marisa. "We are at the grocery store there, Mama is at the checkout, she blows up, drags us out, the groceries they are still there."

"Cooper?" said Du Pré.

Nods.

"She don't get a phone call, nothing?" he said.

Shakes of little heads.

"You don't know nothin'?"

Looks of wide-eyed innocence.

"Somebody pissin' on my boots telling me it is rainin'," said Du Pré.

Looks of wide-eyed injured virtue.

"Pallas kill you, you tell," said Du Pré.

"It's a pret' bad spot be in," said Berne. "That Pallas she is in ver' big trouble."

"She is usually," said Du Pré. "She is that sort of kid."

"Not like this," said Marisa.

"You ain't going, tell me anything?" said Du Pré.

Little palms turned up.

Du Pré looked up the street. Jacqueline was crossing it, striding straight, her arms stiff and swinging.

"OK," said Du Pré, "me, I cannot beat it out of you."

Jacqueline stopped and she glared at Du Pré.

"OK," said Du Pré, "maybe one of you talk I don't tell on you."

"Yeah," said Berne, "but all these guys squeal, soon as Pallas she start in on them. Sorry, Grandpère, it is not worth it."

Du Pré looked up the street again.

Jacqueline was stalking back across the dirt road, on her way to another house.

"She is pissed," said Du Pré.

"We maybe stay at Madelaine's?" said Berne.

"Till this blows over," said Marisa.

Chorus of hopeful yesses!

Du Pré nodded.

"Go ask her," he said.

The kids shot out of the van and raced into the saloon.

I go run with the buffalo, polish the rocks up, my ribs, come home there is something mysterious it is going on, Du Pré thought, I never see my Jacqueline this pissed off.

Du Pré heard a car coming, fast. He turned around. It was one of the tan government sedans. The car raced up and the driver slammed on the brakes.

Ripper.

He jumped out. His eyes were wild.

"Where is that little *shit?*" he screamed.

Du Pré looked at him.

"Pallas?" he said.

Ripper saw Jacqueline up the street. He ran off, yelling.

Harvey was sitting in the passenger seat. He had his face in his hands and he was laughing so hard he was choking.

Du Pré walked round and he stood looking in the open window.

Harvey leaned back, choking.

"What she do?" said Du Pré.

Harvey started to laugh again and he could not speak. Every time he would look at Du Pré he would dissolve again.

Du Pré waited.

Harvey gasped and he mopped his face with his handkerchief. He picked up a folded newspaper that sat on the seat beside him. He handed it to Du Pré.

It was one of those rags you see in supermarkets, with headlines like "Six Hundred Pound Baby Born to Chinese Giants."

This one did not say that. It said, "FBI Agent to Wed Ten-Year-Old."

Du Pré went round and he got in the driver's seat.

"There is a bar in Cooper," Du Pré said. "We go there now a while."

CHAPTER

36

The Mint Saloon in Cooper was a dark and quiet place. The backbar was ornate, the walls covered in mouldering elk, moose, bighorn sheep, and deer heads and racks.

Harvey came back from the bathroom where he had soaked his face in cold water.

"The director loves headlines like those," said Harvey.

"He fire Ripper maybe," said Du Pré.

Harvey shook his head.

"Only if Ripper *did* marry Pallas," said Harvey.

Du Pré shook his head.

"Maybe he better, get it over with," he said.

"That kid," said Harvey, "how the hell she managed that I do not know."

Du Pré sighed. He had a stiff gulp of his ditchwater highball.

"OK," he said, "so what is with the people out there?"

"Nothing," said Harvey. "We're both waiting. No threats, no

shots, no attempts by anyone to escape. We will have to sit there until they come out."

"What if they shoot?" said Du Pré.

Harvey shook his head.

"Even then," he said, "we've had enough trouble. Short of them all charging us, we don't do anything but wait."

Du Pré sighed.

The door opened and a couple of burly ranchers came in. They were dusty and smeared. They were still wearing their roping gloves.

The woman behind the bar looked up and she drew a couple beers.

"How's the buffalo business?" she said.

"We got them sons of bitches stuck off in a box canyon," said one rancher. "I think we'll just shoot 'em."

"Lost four miles of fence my place," said the other. "I'd about sue them kooks over there to the Eide place. Hard to do when they're all surrounded by the feds."

"I'd like to find the peckerhead who started 'em runnin'," said one.

"No shit," said the other.

"String him up by his goddamned nuts," said the one.

The ranchers drank their beer and held out their glasses.

"Oughta just go on in that damn cult's antpile," said the one.

"Lot of children in there," said the woman.

"Them feds'll screw it up," said the one rancher.

"They screw up anything they touch," said the other.

"Amen," said Harvey.

The ranchers gulped their beers and they went back out.

Du Pré sighed.

"Good thing they didn't recognize you, Gabriel," said the woman behind the bar. "Been too busy chasing them buffalo, watch TV that much."

"Yah," said Du Pré, "well, Helen, I did not start that."

"Uh-huh," she said.

"No, it was not me," said Du Pré. "I was chased, this bull buffalo."

"Well," said the woman, "they're raisin' hell with the fences and all and folks around here were pretty fed up with them crazy assholes early on. Come around, they did, tried to buy up some of the ranches here."

"Anybody sell?" said Harvey.

"Not that I know of," said the woman. "Course, nobody'd known that the Eides had either."

Harvey looked at the pressed-tin ceiling. About a thousand fly-specked dollar bills hung from it.

He looked at Du Pré.

Du Pré got up and went over to the bar.

"You know somethin'," he said. "It may be it is dangerous they got another place, no one knows."

Helen looked at him.

"Just rumors," she said, "the Lucas place. They'd been havin' a lot of trouble, making the land payments. I dunno for sure, but . . . well, Lucases used to come in pretty regular and they ain't been. It's that way somebody sells out, you know, they get ashamed."

Du Pré nodded.

Lucas place, couple ranches over from Hulmes, got the water right on Coffee Pot Creek.

Du Pré went back to the table.

"Well," said Harvey, "I guess that we had better go on back. I got this siege to run."

They went out and got in the government sedan. They turned around and headed back toward Toussaint.

"Wonder if they found the little monster yet?" said Harvey.

Du Pré shook his head.

"She won't come out, it is dark," he said. "Pallas is smart and she knows she is in big shit, this."

"I love that kid," said Harvey, "and I thank all the gods she is somebody else's."

Du Pré grinned at him.

"She stir it up good," he said, "ten years old. Me, I maybe live long enough, see her at twenty."

"The mind reels," said Harvey.

Toussaint was visible in the near distance.

A TV helicopter was landing across the road from the saloon.

Du Pré drove on.

He pulled around in back of the saloon.

"I think I'll wait here," said Harvey. "If you happen to see Ripper, tell him I stand ready to be his best man."

Du Pré nodded. He went in the back door of the saloon.

Madelaine was still sitting on her stool behind the bar. Jacqueline and Ripper were down at one end, glowering. A few reporters were off at the tables, drinking and laughing.

Madelaine looked up at Du Pré. She nodded.

"You gutless fuck," she said. She smiled.

Du Pré shrugged.

"These . . ." he said, jerking his head at the reporters.

"Non," said Madelaine. "Just bored, fly around, look at the buildings, there is nothing to see there. Crazy people. Those poor kids."

A cell phone chirred. One of the reporters flipped open the little black dingus. He put it to his ear.

"Let's go," the reporter yelled.

All the people at the tables ran out the door.

Ripper got up and came to Du Pré.

"Where's Harvey?" he said. Du Pré jerked his head toward the back door. Ripper ran out.

Tires squealing. The car roared off very fast.

"Now something," said Madelaine.

Du Pré nodded.

Jacqueline came down to join them. She looked tired.

"Find her?" said Du Pré.

"Non," said Jacqueline, "she is layin' real low. Smart kid."

"Others are all at my house," said Madelaine, "filling sand-bags."

"Ver' funny," said Jacqueline. "You know what that little shit did? She call that cheap newspaper tell them the story. They don't believe her. She got this tape, Ripper, him talking our house where he is. She mess with the tape, having him say things. You know, take a few words here, some there. She play it over the phone, those shits at that paper. Now they are curious. They come here, we don't know it, get the story, everybody knows Pallas, she has decided she is marrying Ripper, a few years she is old enough. So people they say yes, of course, they think it is a big joke . . ."

Du Pré nodded.

Me, I give her that tape recorder she says she wants one, small and good, tape bird calls. I think she means rap music.

Don't bring it up now.

Madelaine laughed.

"Ripper, he is not so happy," she said.

"Me, either," said Jacqueline. "Goddamned kid."

Benny Klein came in. He looked into the gloom and saw Du Pré.

"They're comin' out," said Benny.

Du Pré whirled on his stool.

"Yeah," said Benny. "They're comin' out now, hands over their heads, and all."

Du Pré got up and went out to his cruiser. He started the engine.

"Grandpère," Pallas yelled. "I am in the trunk, you let me out!"

Du Pré ignored her. He drove off fast.

CHAPTER

37

Du Pré parked back away from the police cars and the National Guard carriers.

"Grandpère!" said Pallas.

"You!" said Du Pré, "you be quiet. You stay there I maybe be an hour, more. You are in deep *shit.*"

"OK, Grandpère," said Pallas, in a very small voice.

Du Pré got out. It was cloudy, so Pallas wouldn't bake too badly in the trunk. He walked up toward the searchlights banked on either side of the gate. Harvey and Ripper were there. The armed and armored men around the perimeter were all standing and looking on.

The Host of Yahweh was filing out of the big metal buildings. They blinked in the light. Small children were wailing. The men wore the odd billowy shirts, the women long gray dresses and bonnets. They marched four abreast toward the gate.

Du Pré watched as they walked past, led by cops. The people

were directed to an open meadow and asked to sit.

Du Pré walked up to Harvey and Ripper. Another agent was filming the Host marching out of their compound. Du Pré stared hard at the faces of the men, but he didn't see any he knew.

Some were older, some younger, some of the women had white hair and glasses, some of the men were bald, well into their sixties. Some of them were quite young. All of them were silent.

They filed past in fours, or in families, fathers and mothers carrying little ones or keeping older children in line. The TV cameras were rolling. There was a bank of thirty of them, all with their technicians glued to the eyepieces and sound gauges.

"It would help," said Harvey, in a low voice, "if we had any idea just who we were looking for."

The crowd walked fairly swiftly. The last few people passed, and then the cops began to rush the metal buildings.

"I don't see that guy," said Ripper, "that smoothie who was cutting us up so bad on the tube."

Harvey nodded.

The cops got to the buildings. They had drawn weapons. One opened the door and the others rushed in.

A few minutes passed.

The big sliding doors on the side of one of the buildings were pushed open.

"Search every box bigger'n one for shoes," said Harvey, "for people. After that, search 'em all. Tapes, discs, what-have-you."

A small black dog ran out through the open sliding doors.

Harvey looked at a computer in his hand. He walked over to Du Pré. Faces appeared on the screen. The doctor who had been so eloquent after the woman had killed herself.

Tate.

The avuncular man with the long brown hair who had said that the Host of Yahweh had nothing to hide.

"None of them, at least that I saw," said Harvey.

"Parker?" said Du Pré.

Harvey shook his head.

Du Pré hadn't seen her, either.

Harvey sighed.

"This," he said, "is a fucking mess. We have to bus all these people somewhere and interview all of them."

Du Pré nodded.

"We look like your friendly jackbooted persecutors," said Harvey.

Du Pré nodded.

"This isn't right. Something isn't right," said Harvey.

Du Pré looked at all of the modular homes and trailers. They seemed lifeless. The Host of Yahweh had stayed out of sight in the big metal buildings. Search teams began to go through the homes and the long white double-wides.

Harvey slapped his thigh with his hand.

"Son of a bitch," he said. "Here I sit, waiting for one of them to tell me they've found a dead cop."

Du Pré nodded.

An ambulance started up its sirens and it came roaring up the road and shot down to the compound. The attendants jumped out and grabbed a wheeled stretcher and then went in the sliding doors.

Harvey listened to his radio, the earpiece in.

He frowned.

"Found Parker," he said, "unconscious. Otherwise all right. Jesus Christ."

A medevac helicopter came over low and landed near the metal building. The ambulance attendants wheeled the stretcher out and lifted it into the helicopter. The blades began to swirl faster and the machine lifted up. When it was five hundred feet up, the pilot kicked in the jet engines and soon it was a speck on the horizon.

Du Pré looked over at the houses. Men were dashing in and

out of them, bursting in a door and then appearing on the far side headed for another.

"Maybe they got out," said Du Pré.

Harvey nodded.

"Thing about electronic gear," he said, "is that electronic gear can make it do things it ought not to."

"I will be at Madelaine's," said Du Pré, "or the saloon."

Harvey nodded.

Du Pré walked back down to his cruiser. He opened the trunk.

Pallas blinked at the light.

"You," said Du Pré, "maybe I just shoot you, dump you in a coyote den, let them eat you. Your mama, she get hold of you, she skin you."

Pallas sat up.

"Maybe," she said, "I hide out a while, Madelaine's."

"Madelaine mad at you, too," said Du Pré.

Pallas thought about that.

"I am thirsty," she said.

Du Pré lifted her out.

"OK," he said, "I got some water. Maybe we take you, Benetsee's. You be safe there."

Pallas stumbled a little. Her leg had gone to sleep.

"Hot in there," she said.

Du Pré lifted her up and put her in the front seat. He got the water jug from behind the driver's seat and gave it to her. He got in and started the cruiser and turned it around and drove on back toward the road, the blacktop.

"You are some trouble," said Du Pré. "You make trouble for Ripper, you make trouble, your mother."

Pallas drank water and stayed silent.

She put the cap back on the jug and set it on the floor.

"Yeah," she said. "Me, I did not think they would buy it."

Du Pré nodded.

"Me," he said, "I never see your mother so mad."

"She get plenty mad," said Pallas. "You are not around her then."

"I am around her *now*," said Du Pré. "She bite your head off, piss down your throat she is mad."

Pallas began to cry. She blubbered.

"You," said Du Pré, "quit that shit. I know you. You are not sorry one bit. You got Ripper half crazy, you set him up good."

Pallas quit snuffling. Du Pré turned off on the bench road that led to Benetsee's. Pallas stayed quiet.

"Maybe," said Du Pré, "you leave Montana, maybe you grow a mustache, wear glasses, get a job."

"Where?" said Pallas, weakly.

"Bolivia," said Du Pré. "It is a good place you are Butch Cassidy the Sundance Kid."

Pallas laughed.

"Pret' good movie," she said.

"Yah," said Du Pré. "Remember they get shot to shit the end."

"Yah," said Pallas, "so what I do."

"Hide out, Benetsee's," said Du Pré. "I come get you when Jacqueline she is more worried than she is mad."

"OK," said Pallas.

Du Pré got the cruiser up to speed.

"You!" he yelled.

Pallas looked up at him.

"I am a ver' proud grandpère!" yelled Du Pré.

They laughed and rolled along the dirt road.

CHAPTER
38

"You take that little shit to Benetsee?" said Madelaine. She was sitting in her kitchen, drinking chamomile tea.

Du Pré looked at the ceiling.

"I don't rat her out," said Madelaine. "Jacqueline get a good grip on your nuts you will sing like a capon you don't talk fast."

Du Pré nodded.

"I think," said Madelaine, "maybe I got this idea."

Du Pré looked at her.

"She is like them other kids some, but she got something else, too," said Madelaine. "I talk, her teacher, the school. They got the computers there. Other kids they are doing kid stuff, ten, you know. Learning about science, a little . . ."

Du Pré rolled a smoke.

"Pallas, she is liking math," said Madelaine.

Du Pré nodded.

"You don't got a checking account, Du Pré," said Madelaine.

Du Pré shook his head.

"Now," said Madelaine, "here is this thing, you tell me what it is."

She pushed a sheet of paper over to Du Pré. Du Pré looked at it.

"Them two bars there," he said, nodding, "they are that equal sign."

"Yah," said Madelaine, "so what is the rest of it there?"

Du Pré looked at it.

"Alphabet," said Du Pré.

"Yah," said Madelaine, "what alphabet?"

Du Pré shrugged.

"How many languages you got?" said Madelaine.

Du Pré laughed.

"English, Coyote French," said Du Pré.

"Yah," said Madelaine, "me, too. This is another language, though, Du Pré. What is it?"

Du Pré raised his eyebrows and shook his head.

"Greek," said Madelaine.

"Pallas, she is learning Greek?" said Du Pré.

"Non!" said Madelaine. "I tell you math. Math she is doing has these Greek letters in it."

"Why?" said Du Pré.

Madelaine sipped her tea while Du Pré smoked.

"So I ask the teacher what kind of math is this. She says she don't know. She goes, the computer, asks somebody someplace, they say, it is sort of math, graduate students studying math do, but not very many. Also pretty tough problem you have solved there, so what is this person got maybe a doctorate in math is doing in Toussaint, Montana?"

"Shit," said Du Pré.

"Yah," said Madelaine, "so we shit, us, and we maybe talk to that Bart. Pallas is so smart, we maybe ought to let her do something here."

"Jacqueline, she will not like this," said Du Pré. Jacqueline was a good mother and she loved her children fiercely.

"She be fine," said Madelaine.

Du Pré sighed.

"Maybe Pallas don't want do much anyway," said Du Pré.

Madelaine nodded.

"We ask her," said Madelaine.

Du Pré looked at his watch. He went to the telephone.

Bart answered on the first ring.

"It is me," said Du Pré, "That Pallas is, some math genius. So what the fuck I do."

"What does Pallas want to do?" said Bart.

"I don't ask her yet," said Du Pré.

"Well," said Bart, "ask her, and if she wants to go to some school for it, of course I will pay for it. No problem, any of those kids, they all can go to school on me if they want. You know that."

"I got to ask," said Du Pré.

"So ask her," said Bart, "and then if she wants to do something we can go from there."

"OK," said Du Pré. "Thanks."

"Sure," said Bart. "I got to go, there's somebody at the door."

Du Pré hung up.

"OK," said Madelaine, "so you got to ask Pallas, then Jacqueline."

Du Pré yawned.

Madelaine rapped the table with her knuckles.

"Du Pré," she said. "You go ask Pallas."

"Why?" said Du Pré. "She is there in the morning. Maybe she will forget that Ripper, marry Benetsee. Them, perfect match."

Madelaine snorted.

"God damn it," she said, "you go and do that now."

"Why?" said Du Pré.

"I got this feeling," said Madelaine. "You go to sleep you want to, I go maybe."

Du Pré shrugged, stood up, went to the front hall, took his old leather jacket down from the peg in the wall. He yawned.

Madelaine leaned against the wall.

"I go with you," she said, putting on a heavy sweater she had knitted.

They went out and got in Du Pré's cruiser and he drove out to the bench road. It was very dark. He put his high beams on.

A mule deer bounded across the road. The headlights flared red in its eye.

Du Pré turned into the narrow rutted track that led to Benetsee's cabin and he drove up close and they got out. There was a lamp burning on the little table in front of the window.

Du Pré opened the door.

"Pallas!" he said.

Nothing.

Madelaine went past him.

"Pallas!" she said. "You come out now!"

Some of the clothes on the big shelf moved a little and Pallas looked out, grinning. She slid out. She had a little pistol in her hand.

Madelaine put her hands on her hips.

"Where you get that?" she said. "Give that, me, now."

Pallas meekly handed it to her, butt first. Madelaine pulled back the slide. A bullet tapped on the floor.

"Where you get this?" she said.

"I find it," said Pallas.

"In the box, the tractor," said Du Pré.

"What goddamn tractor?" said Madelaine.

"The one the house," said Du Pré. "It is for snakes, maybe mice you are plowing. Got birdshot, the shells."

Madelaine pulled out the clip. She pressed the spring and five shells popped into her hand.

"Hollow points," said Madelaine. "Birdshot, horseshit."

Pallas was looking at the floor while she edged toward the door.

"Where you get these?" said Madelaine, holding out the .22 shells.

"Gopher bullets," said Pallas.

Du Pré was trying to keep his face straight.

"You going to shoot, gopher, behind the clothes?" said Madelaine.

"I don't know it is you," said Pallas.

"Where is Benetsee?" said Madelaine.

"The sweat," said Pallas.

Madelaine relaxed.

"You see him?" she said.

Pallas nodded.

"OK," said Madelaine, "so what is this?"

Pallas looked up at her.

"Benetsee say I got to hide someone come," she said. "I don't know why."

"Jacqueline," said Madelaine, "him tell you, hide, her?"

Pallas nodded.

"Bullshit," said Madelaine. "You . . . little shit. You got something, you are doing."

Du Pré went outside so he could laugh.

"You answer me, you listen, me, you little shit," said Madelaine. "I tan your ass, make coin purses out of it."

"OK, OK," said Pallas. "Ripper, well, what if he needs help?"

"Non!" said Madelaine. "You are ten!"

"I know that," said Pallas.

"What you do? Shoot bad guys shooting at Ripper?"

"Maybe," said Pallas.

Du Pré went back in. He knelt down.

"Look, you," he said, "you are ver' good that math. You want maybe go to a school, does that?"

"Sure," said Pallas.

"We talk to Bart," said Du Pré, "and we talk to Jacqueline."

Pallas grinned.

"Johns Hopkins," she said. "I go there."

Madelaine looked down at the little girl. She looked at Du Pré.

"Baltimore," she said. "It is ver' close I hear to that Washington, D.C."

Du Pré nodded.

"Come on," he said, and he picked up Pallas and carried her to the cruiser.

Du Pré parked in front of his old house where Jacqueline and Raymond and their brood lived now. Pallas looked at her grandfather.

"You make a run for it, Grandpère," she said. "I am that dead meat anyway."

The front door opened.

Jacqueline came down the steps. Pallas got out of the car and slammed the door and Du Pré punched the accelerator and roared off, laughing.

He drove to Bart's, and up the long drive. Someone was staggering down the road. Booger Tom. He had a hand to his head.

Du Pré stopped and got out.

"Bart's gone," said Booger Tom.

"Who?" said Du Pré.

Booger Tom looked at the blood on his hand.

"Can't say," he said. "I was sleepin', you see."

CHAPTER

39

Du Pré watched the Host of Yahweh return. He sat in his old cruiser by the gravel road as the blue-and-white vans went by. New vans, with California plates.

He shook his head.

"Fucked, ain't it?" said Ripper. He was wearing worn ranch clothes and had a battered hat pulled down low. "Not a thing we could do. Parker was in the goddamn *infirmary*. Best of care and all that. And the quacks in Billings can't figure what the hell is wrong with her, other'n viral meningitis. She's delirious."

Du Pré spat out the window.

"How is Harvey?" he said.

"Shitting warty pickles," said Ripper. "You know, shootout with eleven women up to no good, who kill themselves, and nothing in the truck or the van that ties them to anyone here. Yeah, obviously they belonged with this mob. But one of them owned the van and another leased the truck. We got dick. Squat."

"What about the mine," said Du Pré, "the weapons?"

"Oh, that," said Ripper. "Well, the two guys were there are dead, the shit was all blown to hell, and . . . no way to prove that anyone in the Host knew it was there. They have lawyers. They have lots of lawyers. We just can't arrest folks 'less we got a *reason*. Can't just pitch the lot of them in the dungeon. I mean, they are *good*. They fuck up, they die. They make *themselves* die."

"You don't ask questions?" said Du Pré.

"Of course we did," said Ripper, "like, these eleven murderous broads were coming here. Why?"

"They say *we don't know*," said Du Pré.

"They say that for a while, then they all scream HABEAS CORPUS and that is that. The stolen weapons were here, all right, trouble is we can't prove they got here after the Host got here. We looked for any kind of evidence. Fingerprints. Hair. You blew the shit out of all of that, too."

"Owner, the ranch, arrest him the weapons," said Du Pré.

"Owner, the ranch, a corporation, officers unknown."

"Unknown?" said Du Pré.

"Names," said Ripper, "don't match any of the names here. California, either. They have a place in Maine, too. North Carolina."

Du Pré rolled a smoke.

"Parker," he said.

"Parker," said Ripper, "cute little blonde. Now she may not make it through. Viral meningitis, very nasty stuff."

"How she get it?" said Du Pré.

"They gave it to her somehow," said Ripper, "is how. But what it is we do not know. How they gave it to her we do not know. Why no one else has it we do not know."

Du Pré nodded.

"So back they come. We did not find so much as an out-of-date *prescription* in there. I shoulda planted some evidence," said Ripper. "I shoulda done it."

"Like what?" said Du Pré.

"That was where I got stuck. I hear all the time how we jackbooted government swine plant evidence, convict innocent folk. So maybe I put a couple packets of heroin in one of their bathrooms or something. Then we arrest a few hundred people. Judge would love that. I can see that son of a bitch in Billings. 'You clowns get outta my courtroom,' he would say."

Du Pré laughed.

"Tain't funny," said Ripper. "Usually, we deal with a low form of scum who can be persuaded to screw their buddies, for less time in the joint. Works real good. On them. These folks up and shoot themselves before we can start in. I mean, it is fucking seamless."

"The White Priest," said Du Pré.

"Ah, yes," said Ripper. "Would that we knew who he *was*."

"You got a name," said Du Pré.

"Sure do," said Ripper, "and when we ask the nice computer for all it knows about that name, it knows only that Gary Carl Smith was born 9–21–48, has a Social Security number, and he's never been in trouble."

Du Pré waited.

"That's *all*," said Ripper. "Gary Carl Smith, if we got the right one, never filed a tax return, had a driver's license, or bought a vehicle or property requiring deed or registration. Right away we figure that somebody is using Gary Carl Smith's name, and that Gary Carl Smith lived just long enough to get a Social Security number. Somebody got his name and he has not been using it ever since. Thing is, there are no *tracks*. He gets the Social Security number and never uses it."

Du Pré nodded.

"He is not, here in America, then," said Du Pré.

"We thought of that, too," said Ripper, "and by the way there is no death certificate for a Gary Carl Smith who fits. There are and were a lot of Gary Carl Smiths in America."

Du Pré nodded.

"Sooooo," said Ripper, "we haven't the foggiest what he looks like, we got no fingerprints, dear old mother with baby pictures, high school yearbook, nothing."

More vans went past. They all had heavily tinted windows. The people in them were vague shadows.

"The guys who were killed, the eight o'clock murders," said Ripper, "we couldn't find connections with the eleven women. I mean, man, this is fanaticism. Fanatics have to have a leader. A führer. They have to *see* El Máximo."

"No," said Du Pré.

"No?" said Ripper.

"This guy," said Du Pré, "he got to have people put his tapes, the machine, say his words, get his messages. Those people, they are one step away, being the leader."

Ripper waved away Du Pré's cigarette smoke.

"OK," he said.

"That is it," said Du Pré.

"What?" said Ripper.

Du Pré shook his head. He started the engine and looked in the mirror and then he wheeled around and headed back toward town.

He drove up behind the saloon and went to the double room that Pidgeon was in. He rapped on the door.

Pidgeon opened it. Three computer screens were on, and there was a smell of electricity and perfume that wafted out of the door.

"Where is that Harvey?" said Du Pré.

"He had to go to Billings," said Pidgeon.

"Call him," said Du Pré.

"Talk," said Pidgeon.

Du Pré shook his head.

"Come in," said Pidgeon. "Send that one off to wash that crappy old car of yours. With a fucking toothbrush."

"She looooooooovvvves me," said Ripper.

They went in. An air conditioner was humming and the air was cool and dry. Pidgeon motioned to a couple of chairs. Du Pré sat and so did Ripper.

"What?" said Pidgeon.

"I am not sure," said Du Pré. "Tate, the guy who was in the robes, him, who are they?"

Pidgeon went to her files and pulled a couple of folders out. She handed them to Du Pré.

"Guys who are killed," said Du Pré.

More folders. Du Pré went through them slowly. He nodded once or twice.

"I need to talk that Foote," said Du Pré.

"You have a number?" said Pidgeon.

Du Pré fished it out of his wallet.

Pidgeon punched numbers in her cell phone. She put it to her ear. She looked at Du Pré. She handed the phone to him.

"Leave your message," said Foote's voice.

"I am at . . ." Du Pré looked at Pidgeon. She took the phone and said her numbers twice.

"I wish," said Ripper, "I knew what the fuck was going on."

Du Pré nodded.

"I am not sure," said Du Pré, "but I am maybe right."

"What?" said Ripper, exasperated.

The cell phone trilled. Pidgeon answered.

"Oh, you," said Pidgeon.

She handed the phone to Du Pré.

"What's up?" said Harvey.

"I think of something," said Du Pré. "This Gary Carl Smith."

"The White Priest," said Harvey.

"You don't know him," said Du Pré, "what he looks like."

"No," said Harvey. "Guy's completely buried. Invisible."

"No," said Du Pré, "him dead. He has been dead a long time."

"Christ," said Harvey.

"First place this Host of Yahweh has," said Du Pré.

"Christ," said Harvey. "The Lucas farm."

Somebody banged on the door.

"I'll see about it," said Harvey.

Du Pré shut the phone up.

Pidgeon went to the door. Booger Tom was standing there. He looked at Pidgeon appreciatively.

"Doo Pray," said Booger Tom. "Where's that fat wop?"

CHAPTER

40

"This better be one good hunch," said Ripper. "One very good hunch."

Du Pré nodded. He looked down at the Lucas place from a line of trees on a knee of the mountain. The green mercury lamp that threw light on the dirt turnaround between the house and the two barns and the sheds was blazing.

"Who answered the phone?" said Ripper.

"Mrs. Lucas," said Du Pré, "said she had flu. Wasn't feeling good. Lucas, gone to Dakota to look at a combine."

"They haven't got enough wheat to need one," said Ripper.

Du Pré nodded.

"Harvey thinks you're nuts," said Ripper.

Du Pré shook his head.

"Bart is there, Tate is there, that other guy is there, couple more maybe. Lucases are dead, probably."

"Well," said Ripper, "I am going to wriggle down there and peek in the window."

Du Pré shook his head.

"No," he said, "we go to the ditch there, road passes by. They got to move, now, by this morning maybe they find Gary Carl Smith, then everything comes apart."

"Yes," said Ripper. "It do, it do."

Du Pré looked back toward the county road. A pair of headlights was coming east on it. The car slowed and turned on to the ranch road. It speeded up.

"Right on time," said Ripper.

"OK," said Du Pré, "they maybe got some electronic stuff. We don't get too close."

"If they come out we get close," said Ripper.

Du Pré nodded.

Ripper moved down the path quickly, young and agile. Du Pré kept up, hurting here and there.

The car pulled into the brightly lit area.

The cop cruiser stopped dead in the middle of the lot. It was not a terribly big lot, and electrical lines crowded one end of it. Benny Klein got out and looked around for a moment, then walked to the front door of the house and knocked. He waited for a moment and then knocked again, hard.

Du Pré and Ripper were a few feet up the hill, and they could hear Benny's knuckles on the door.

Du Pré grabbed Ripper's arm.

"No dogs," he said, "so they are there all right."

"Bastards," said Ripper.

Benny banged a third time and then walked back to his cruiser and got in and put on all of the lights, and he stepped swiftly out and had a shotgun to his shoulder. He fired twice and the mercury lamp blew up and there were only the lights from the car. Benny ran toward the machine shed, directly back of the cruiser.

Du Pré looked to the south. Running lights. The helicopter was coming on fast, and then it slowed.

"Now," said Du Pré, and he began to run. He had the MP-40 that Catfoot had smuggled back from Europe in his hands.

A man dressed in black, his face behind a ski mask, ran out the front door of the house, toward the cruiser. He was moving fast, and Du Pré lifted up the machine pistol and fired and the man was knocked off his feet and he sprawled in the dirt.

The helicopter was getting closer. It slowed and a beam of light stabbed down from it. The beam was set on the front door of the house, which was open.

Then it shut.

Du Pré and Ripper got to the house. Du Pré picked up a brick and threw it through the picture window in the back, where the kitchen was. Ripper had two concussion grenades armed and he tossed them in and they crouched below the window.

Crump crump.

Ripper vaulted through the hole where the picture window had been. Du Pré went round to the door in the side of the house and he waited. The door opened and a man stumbled out. He was handcuffed and his mouth was taped. Another man, all in black, came right behind.

Du Pré pressed the trigger and the point-blank burst lifted the man up and shoved him a good ten feet.

Du Pré slammed into Bart and knocked him down behind the pile of stove wood near the garden. Then he pointed the MP-40 at the doorway.

It was an empty black hole.

The helicopter circled. The beam began to come close to Du Pré and Bart. Du Pré turned his back so the pilot could see the silver reflective tape on the jacket. The beam held them for just a second and then it went back to probing the house.

Du Pré pulled off his gloves. He found an end on the duct tape and pulled.

"Thanks," Bart gasped. "They have something in there. It's in a small refrigerator. Runs off a battery or a plug."

"They give you shots?" said Du Pré.

Bart nodded.

"We get you out of here in a hurry," said Du Pré.

Someone was tumbling out of the door. Du Pré held the machine pistol on him, and then the beam of light from the helicopter shone down and Du Pré saw the tape.

Ripper kept rolling until he was by the woodpile.

"They went out a window," said Ripper. "Fucking arsenal in there."

A burst of automatic fire reached up toward the helicopter and the searchlight went out and the big machine sheered off. The sliding doors on the barn opened and a stream of fire chewed out the lights of the police cruiser.

Whines. Small engines.

Two little four-wheel ORVs roared out of the dark. Du Pré raised his MP-40. Ripper shoved the barrel down.

"We need them alive," said Ripper. "We have no idea yet what goddamn disease they're giving out. Jesus Christ, you think they'd have the good taste to stick to nerve gas."

The little ORVs were moving down the road that cut east of the Hulme place.

Headed for the *malpais*, the badlands.

Du Pré stood up.

"Son a bitch," he said.

"Stay away from Bart," said Ripper. He took out a foil packet, tore it open, and handed the white folded square to Bart.

"Put it on," said Ripper. "We'll get you out of here to a hospital in a few minutes."

Bart unfolded the mask and put it over his nose and mouth and tied the strings behind his head. The knot wouldn't hold. Du Pré went to him and fixed it snug but not tight, with a double pull.

There were several helicopters now, and they began to come down in the pastures to the west and north and east. Men in moon suits stepped out of them and began to walk toward the house.

Ripper and Du Pré and Bart waited for them, but they didn't stop. They switched on flashlights and went in and in a moment lights began to come on in the house.

Du Pré patted Bart on the shoulder. Bart looked at him. He shook his head.

"There are people at the Hulmes'?" said Du Pré to Ripper.

Ripper shook his head.

"Not enough men," he said.

"Jesus!" said Du Pré.

"We got them out," said Ripper. "I mean, Benny's deputies were going to. Our guys should get there before those shits do."

Du Pré relaxed.

Ripper walked to the man Du Pré had killed. He pulled off the ski mask. Du Pré went over. It was the affable bearded man who had claimed to be the White Priest.

"Who is he?" said Du Pré.

Ripper shook his head.

"Milford, maybe," he said. "Pidgeon could tell you."

Jet turbines whined.

"Here's your ride," said Ripper. He patted Bart on the shoulder.

A black Humvee came roaring up the road and braked to a skidding stop and three men got out.

"Come on," said Ripper, grabbing Du Pré's arm, "this is our ride."

The driver of the Humvee started to say something.

"Indianapolis," said Ripper.

The man backed away.

Du Pré got in and so did Ripper.

"Like my momma said," said Ripper, "if you got something on everybody, you got something."

He headed for the *malpais*.

The barbed wire fence twanged when he drove through it.

"Motherfuckers!" screamed Ripper.

CHAPTER
41

The Humvee lurched down into a dry wash. The shocks and springs were so good that Du Pré lifted himself clear out of his seat bracing for a hard shock that never came.

"*Arnold Schwarzenegger!*" screamed Ripper. "*Arnold drives these suckers!*"

Ripper roared up the wash, the Humvee going impossibly fast on the rough ground.

"It makes me want to invade something," said Ripper, "Ireland, Iraq, Indiana . . . some foreign land."

The two ORVs were a mile or so ahead, bouncing wildly on the rocky flat. Ripper closed the gap. When he was two hundred yards away from the two ORVs the men on them looked back and made a skidding turn and headed for a butte surrounded by slabs of pale ocher rock.

The Humvee could not follow very far. Ripper jumped out after popping open the rear door. He opened a plastic chest and fished out flak jackets and a couple of machine pistols.

"Heckler and Koch," said Ripper. "Light and vicious. And these are what to feed them."

He handed Du Pré some clips. Du Pré dropped the flak jacket and put the clips in the pockets of his old buckskin coat.

Ripper nodded. He dropped his flak jacket and unzipped his fly and pissed on it.

"Regulations demand I wear it," he said. "I must write myself up after all this. Those assholes are going to scramble up there and we will go after them. I am afraid, Du Pré, afraid. Are there rattlesnakes in these rocks?"

"No," said Du Pré.

"Lying sack of shit," said Ripper.

Something went *craaack!* and they both hit the ground.

"They have a rifle," said Ripper.

Two more reports and a hole appeared in the Humvee's windshield.

"*More paperwork,*" screamed Ripper. "*I hate paperwork. You pricks will pay for this!*"

Two more shots.

"A .223," said Ripper. "They couldn't hit a bull in the ass if they leaned up against him. It is why we lost the last few wars."

Ripper was in the lee of a slab of rock, and Du Pré behind a giant boulder. Ripper waved his hat. Another shot, ricocheting off the stone.

"Enough," said Ripper. He wriggled to the rear of the Humvee and fished around and wriggled back with two plastic tubes.

"OK," said Du Pré, "you think you cannot hit anything, the .223, I shoot a couple of those, they are worse."

"They have been *improved,*" said Ripper. "The tactics are the usual."

"Asshole," said Du Pré.

"You could shoot this," said Ripper, "or we could draw straws."

"You call it," said Du Pré.

"One, two, three," said Ripper.

Du Pré stood up and fired an entire clip of ammunition at the jumbled rocks above. He ran to the right, keeping his eyes on the slope.

He saw a movement and ducked behind a rock. Ripper fired the plastic bazooka and the rocket screeched toward the slope. It burst and gravel spattered the boulders.

"Go," said Ripper.

Du Pré dashed from stone to boulder to a knee of rock and peeked through a crack.

Nothing moved.

"Didn't bite this time," said Ripper.

"I go round," said Du Pré. "There is a way up maybe they can't see."

Ripper nodded and set down the bazooka and picked up the machine pistol. He popped up and sprayed the slope.

Du Pré ran, hunched over, and he got far enough away from where the two men were so he didn't have to dodge and stop. He slid behind a ragged ridge that reached up toward the butte's high walls and then began to move up. Du Pré scrambled for two or three minutes and then paused, listening. Ripper would fire a burst and Du Pré would climb.

A huge raven flew past and gave one croaking *cawwwwww.*

Du Pré stopped when he got to the steep walls that fell away from the flat top of the butte. He edged back and over the spine of rock, rolling behind some rubble.

Another rocket hissed and crackled through the air and the warhead burst on a boulder and more bits of rock flew through the air.

Du Pré carefully slid flat stones on top of each other, very slowly, and then peered through the openings.

He waited.

Nothing.

Then there was a small flicker of movement. A man's head began to rise up from behind a rock. He was looking over

243

toward Du Pré. Du Pré slid the barrel of the machine pistol into a big opening in the rocks he had piled.

The man ducked back down.

Ripper fired another burst. Du Pré sighted the machine pistol on the place he had seen the man's head.

He heard a shot.

The man stood up then, trembling violently, his arms jumping around.

"Shit!" said Du Pré. He dashed along the slope toward the shaking man, who then went boneless and fell.

Another shot.

"*Fuck me runnin'*," yelled Ripper. "They did it again, God damn it."

Du Pré edged up to the fallen man. He was lying on his back. His crotch was soiled. There was a little blood at the corner of his mouth. And a lot more on the rocks beneath his head.

Du Pré sighed. He looked down the slope to see Ripper hopping from boulder to boulder. Then he stopped.

"Yours dead?" yelled Ripper.

"Yah," said Du Pré.

"Mine, too," said Ripper. "These assholes don't play fair."

Du Pré slung the machine pistol around his neck and hauled the dead man up by his shirt.

"Leave him," said Ripper. "The evidence techs need work, too."

Du Pré slid and scrambled down the slope.

Ripper looked gray. "These people," he said, "are truly scary."

Du Pré nodded.

"And I am scared," Ripper added.

They walked to the Humvee. Ripper drove Du Pré to Bart's. They got out.

"Wanna couple plastic bazookas?" said Ripper.

Du Pré snorted.

"Well," said Ripper, "I had to ask."

CHAPTER

42

They walked away from the little cemetery and went to Du Pré's old cruiser.

It was raining, cold and gray, and the wind pushed the water hard. Du Pré started the engine and turned on the blower so the windshield would dry off.

Pidgeon was crying. Ripper patted her on the shoulder.

"God damn them, god damn them," said Pidgeon. "She was a brave woman."

Officer Parker had died of the strange virus. Bart had pulled through, but he was still in the hospital. They had him isolated and they were taking no chances.

"We've figured for years that this would happen," said Pidgeon, "but it seemed likely that it would be Iraq or some other psycho country. But it was right here. Homegrown American stuff."

Du Pré pressed the accelerator a little and the volume of

hot air strengthened. He put the cruiser in reverse and backed and turned and he headed north.

Officer Parker had grown up on a ranch south of Miles City. She now slept with her people, under some Siberian elms near a little spring. 1972–2000 it said on the stone under her name.

They didn't speak for a while.

"Those bastards," said Pidgeon again, "you damn near get them and they eat their guns. They are *nuts.*"

The mysterious refrigerator held nothing at all.

The virus that had destroyed Parker's brain was new. It had never been seen before. It resembled other viruses but it wasn't one of the ones catalogued.

"I wonder if the bones they found were Gary Carl Smith's?" said Pidgeon. "I wonder if the three men dead that night were really the ones who ran this thing."

"We busted them all," said Ripper, "every damn one of them, and we are going to keep them and talk to them until somebody cracks."

Pidgeon looked at him.

"What if none of them knows anything?" she said. "What if this was so well done nobody knows anything?"

"Somebody has to know something," said Ripper.

"They don't have to," said Pidgeon.

"I was just trying to be cheerful," said Ripper.

Du Pré got to the Interstate and headed west. The rain was lifting.

"Bart is going to be OK," said Madelaine. "That is something. So now you don't know much. But that virus had to come from someplace. They bought it. You said they did anyway."

"Goddamn Russians," said Pidgeon. "Place falls apart and all that biological weaponry is for sale. Shit, if you wanted to do America in, all you have to do is install smallpox."

Madelaine looked at her.

"That is gone, I thought," she said.

"No," said Pidgeon, "it was wiped out in the population. But we kept some of the virus and the Russians kept some of it. Nobody has been vaccinated for it in twenty-five years. The vaccine wears off in ten. Smallpox starts someplace, way it works it could kill a third of the people in America in maybe two months. There wouldn't be a whole lot we could do. Antibiotics won't touch it."

"Vaccine?" said Madelaine.

"Don't have any," said Pidgeon, "takes a while to make some. So the dickheads in the government, they *hope* it doesn't get out."

"On their watch," said Ripper.

Du Pré snorted.

"Largest criminal conspiracy indictment ever," said Pidgeon, "and the civil libertarians are going batshit. The threat is real. Both of them. To our lives and to our rights. I don't like any of this."

"Grim," said Ripper.

"Shit," said Pidgeon, "if we have to be safe we will pay a big price."

"Maybe it is not so bad," said Du Pré, "maybe you are fighting hard but in the wrong way."

Pidgeon frowned.

"Wrong way?" she said. "We had to find the sons of bitches, had to find out how they did what they did."

Du Pré shook his head.

"How do people, Host of Yahweh, Moonies, them, hold on to people?" he said. "Catholic Church, too."

"The religious compulsions of man," said Ripper.

"Everybody got them," said Du Pré.

Pidgeon waved her hand.

Du Pré laughed and he rolled a cigarette and lit it and he passed it to Madelaine and she took a big drag and passed it to Pidgeon who took one and Ripper cracked his window and gagged and choked and sneezed.

"Put this fucker on the roof," said Pidgeon. "Fucking wimp."

"I have a good yup fetish about my health," said Ripper, "you know, low-fat diet, lots of oat bran. Thing about us yups is that though we know in theory everybody has to die, we know we are so wonderful that an exception will be made in our case. Doctor Spock told our parents that."

"Jesus," said Madelaine, "what crap."

Pidgeon looked at Ripper.

"Spock did not say that," she said.

Ripper looked crestfallen.

"Well," he whined, "he *should* have."

Pidgeon blew smoke in his face.

"You wanna play, we'll play," said Ripper, pulling a small, vile-looking black cigar from his pocket.

"Damn you," said Pidgeon.

"Floor show is over," said Ripper. "Du Pré was saying that the way to fight a spiritual war is with spiritual weapons."

"No shit," said Pidgeon.

"I get it," said Ripper. He leaned forward, lit a match and held it in front of the cigar, which began to glow.

"Get what?" said Pidgeon.

"I get *it!*" said Ripper.

"Get what?" said Pidgeon. "You figure out Du Pré's mysticism is what got us to the Lucas place? Harvey and I have been following that for some time. He gets it from that old son of a bitch Benetsee, who gets it from another world."

Ripper nodded.

"How did you know it was the Lucas place they were at?" said Ripper.

"I am twelve," said Du Pré, "me, I get this new rifle, .30-30 just before deer season. Catfoot, my papa, he give it to me, and he take me to Grandpère Du Pré, who is ver' old, cannot walk much any more and so he will not hunt. Catfoot he leave me there with Grandpère who makes us tea. We drink tea, he says, 'So you hunt deer,' and I say, 'Yes,' and he says, 'So you know how to hunt these deer?' and I say, 'Yes' and he says, 'How is that you hunting deer?"

Du Pré rolled himself a smoke and lit it.

"I say, Grandpère, I go where there are deer, I find a place got wind to my face, I can see their trails, I sit ver' quiet, wait, deer come."

Pidgeon had her arms around herself and she was looking down at the floor and listening very hard. Madelaine was looking at Du Pré and smiling a little.

"Grandpère he look at me a long time. He say, that is bullshit you are saying. Where you get that, those dumb magazines, lie around the barbershop? They are for city people, long way from the deer."

Du Pré turned on the road north, the road home.

"I am feeling foolish," said Du Pré. "My grandpère he don't think much of me, deer hunter, and here I read all those magazines, the barbershop, Catfoot's cousin Henri has it, you know. I have been hunting deer with Catfoot, I am six or so, help him butcher them out, sit with him while he wait for them. So I don't know what I say wrong and I am sad."

Madelaine rubbed Du Pré's shoulder.

"So my grandpère, he leans over, he takes my shoulders, his hands, he says, you got to go, the deer's land, yes, do them things you talk about, the magazines, but it is not the most important thing."

Pidgeon looked up.

"My grandpère, he lean close, put his mouth, my ear, say *hunter, him dream the deer and the deer, him come.*"

Ripper blew foul cigar smoke at Pidgeon.

He turned back to Du Pré.

"If you hadn't thought of the Lucas place," said Ripper, "they might have gotten away. Left the Lucases and Bart dead, too, in the house. Burned it, would have taken a long time to figure out. They were there waiting for the helicopter. If it came, they would have shot Bart and left then."

"Yah," said Du Pré.

"You dreamed this?" said Pidgeon.

Du Pré looked off toward the western horizon.

"Ah," he said, pointing with his thumb, "there is a coyote, by them tree."

"Why don't we ask him?" said Pidgeon.

"Hah," said Du Pré, "coyote, him a trickster, but I know what he say. He say what you hunt is an idea. It got no flesh to kill, got no one to talk to. But you wait, it will wear out."

Pidgeon laughed.

"Bad ideas they wear out," said Du Pré. "That coyote say that."